POWERFUL AND STINGING
SHORT FICTION FROM
BRUCE BENDERSON

"Family Romance"—a depressed suburban father follows his illegally adopted son into drug addiction

"A Visit from Mom"—a young man drifts into a dangerous sexual encounter, all the while worrying that his visiting mother is getting home safely in her good wool suit.

"Intern's Incantation"—a medical intern slips into a halucinatory monologue in a hospital's AIDS ward.

"Stations of the Cross"—a false priest desperately vies for the love of a runaway.

"Recommendations for the Mass Production of Teenagers"—a biting and grimly humorous satire on the institution of child-raising.

PRETENDING TO SAY NO

BRUCE BENDERSON is the author of numerous short stories that have been published in various literary magazines and anthologies, including BETWEEN C&D (Viking). He has translated several French literary works into English. He lives in New York City.

PRETENDING TO SAY NO,

A Novella
and
Eleven Stories

Bruce Benderson

A PLUME BOOK

PLUME
Published by the Penguin Group
Penguin Books USA Inc., 375 Hudson Street,
New York, New York 10014, U.S.A.
Penguin Books Ltd, 27 Wrights Lane, London W8 5TZ, England
Penguin Books Australia Ltd, Ringwood, Victoria, Australia
Penguin Books Canada Ltd, 2801 John Street, Markham, Ontario, Canada L3R 1B4
Penguin Books (N.Z.) Ltd, 182-190 Wairau Road, Auckland 10, New Zealand

Penguin Books Ltd, Registered Offices: Harmondsworth, Middlesex, England

First published by Plume, an imprint of Penguin Books USA Inc.
Published simultaneously in Canada.

First Printing, April, 1990
10 9 8 7 6 5 4 3 2 1

Acknowledgments

Several of the stories in this collection, some in slightly different form, appeared in the following magazines or anthologies: "Pretending to Say No" (as "Brand X") and "Intern's Incantation" in *Central Park*, copyright © 1988 by Neword Productions, Inc.; "A Visit from Mom," "Suicide Ecstasy," and "Dust, Angel" (as "Wheel of Fire") in *Between C & D*, copyright © 1986, 1987, 1988 by Between C & D; "Stations of the Cross" in *Maatstaf* and in *Gin & Comics*, copyright © 1989 by Gin and Comix; "A Black-Boxes Alibi" in *Maatstaf*; and "She" in *The Fiction Review*, copyright © 1988 by Black Lung Press.

 REGISTERED TRADEMARK—MARCA REGISTRADA

LIBRARY OF CONGRESS CATALOGING IN PUBLICATION DATA

Benderson, Bruce.
    Pretending to say no : a novella and eleven stories / Bruce Benderson.
        p.   cm.
    ISBN 0-452-26390-5
    I. Title.
PS3552.E5386P7   1990
813'.54—dc20   89-29471
                                                                             CIP

Printed in the United States of America
Set in Times Roman
Designed by Nissa Knuth

PUBLISHER'S NOTE
This is a work of fiction. Names, characters, places, and incidents either are the product of the author's imagination or are used fictitiously, and any resemblance to actual persons, living or dead, events, or locales is entirely coincidental.

BOOKS ARE AVAILABLE AT QUANTITY DISCOUNTS WHEN USED TO PROMOTE PRODUCTS OR SERVICES.
FOR INFORMATION PLEASE WRITE TO PREMIUM MARKETING DIVISION, PENGUIN BOOKS USA INC.,
375 HUDSON STREET, NEW YORK, NEW YORK 10014.

To bludgeoned Times Square,
to the lacerated city
and to 3 urban friends:
Anthony Colon, Ursule Molinaro, and Scott Neary

Contents

PRETENDING
TO SAY
NO

Pretending to Say No

I'm not shitting you, man, and why should I be? She came, she came to our house! No, really, the buzzer rings and I tell myself, I'm not answering that shit cause if somebody wants to see me they call first. I only answer that bell when I know who it is! But the bell keeps ringing and ringing and Tito, that's my uncle trying to sleep, says, Answer the fucking bell and tell them if they touches it one more time I'm going to blow 'em away! Me in my drawers yet. Who's going to run downstairs five flights to give 'em that message? So I press the buzzer, listen for the door and shouts, You got the wrong place whoever you fucking are, stop leaning on that bell unless you want to get blown away! Let me in, a white-lady voice calls up the stairwell, It's me, Nancy Reagan.

No shit, man. It was the President's wife coming to see us. So I ask Tito, Quick, you know Nancy Reagan? 'Cause since he got involved with those Colombians and started to deal the crack he has contact with some very swift people. They got limousines and everything. And he half asleep saying, Sure, I used to fuck her but her ass was too tight. No, I says, the President's wife.

Yes, it's the President's wife, comes the white-lady voice right at the door this time, Would you please open up for a minute? And my uncle, hearing it too, sits right up in the bed: I gonna knock that damn fool head right off those shoulders if you brought that white drag queen up here, what's her name. No, I says, I didn't tell no drag queen to come up here! I didn't bring no drag queen up here except

1

maybe once. And it was Tito got me to know them, always running crack for him to this bar near the Deuce, and some of those queens, really, listen, if you was standing right next to one of them you might think she was real.

So I walk real quiet to the door, on tippytoes, and take a good look through the peephole. It's a white lady for sure, it ain't no drag queen. For one things this one's too old, and real skinny. She's not wearing no coat and she's got a red dress on. What you want? I call through the door. I just want to come in for a moment, she says and sticks her hand in her purse, pulls out bills and waves them at the peephole. She got money, I tell my uncle. Oh shit, says he, some white bitch coming in the middle of the night to buy crack. But don't let her in now, say I ain't got none. Come back tomorrow, I call through the door. Please, she says. We ain't got nothing, lady, go away.

Then she starts banging on the door real loud, louder than Mr. T. can hit a door, so my uncle gets really pissed and telling China Sue his Chinese chick that he in bed with, Mama, you roll yourself up in this quilt here, and cover your head, ok? 'cause I going to open the door, and he went and got the shotgun. Ok, he goes, Now when I give the sign, you throw the door open, one, two, three, go! He aims the gun and I throw open the door. Wait! goes the white lady, don't do it! I come as a friend. I ain't going to shoot you if you moves your ass out this building now, lady, I ain't got no scotty and I don't want no trouble from the super. Hear me, please, for a second, says she. Who sent you here? says Tito. I just rang any bell. What you doing that for? I need help . . . Now wait a minute, lady, if I let you in, what you going to do? I'll even pay you. She waves the bills at us again, and the top one at least, well that's a twenty. Tito keeps the gun on her but motions with his shoulder. Get in here and put the money on the table.

Nancy Reagan gives a sigh of relief, comes in and puts the money on the table. Tito picks it up. Now what else you got in that purse? Give it here. Oh there's no need for that, she says, your kindness will be rewarded. I've just come from

Odyssey House. Do you know what that is? The drug program? I says. Nancy Reagan smiles and at that moment I know it's her.

So I tell Tito, Yo, Man, this ain't no crack head, this be Nancy Reagan. Tito looks at her close and says, C'mon, man, I told you before if you be bringing those drag queens here from the Deuce you got to tell me first. You can't trust a drag queen, they into stealing and acting like some kind of grand lady, that's what they are all about. Now you got to go 'cause I don't want my nephew hanging out with drag queens.

Yo, man, this ain't a drag queen, you be making a big mistake.

Tito takes another look at her and then he calls Suzy. Tito trusts her about some things. So China Sue comes out and Tito says, Suzy, this a drag queen? Oh my god, Suzy goes, and runs back to the bedroom and puts a sheet on.

So Tito puts down the gun and he kind of bows to her and says, How you doin', Nancy Reagan?

Not so well, says she, since you ask. Maybe you happened to watch TV tonight? Yeah, I did, says Tito, what that got to do with it? Well, says Nancy, didn't you notice what happened to me? Oh, I saw it, pipes up Sue, coming back with the sheet wrapped around her. You were at the drug program and you put your arm around this little black kid and he told the TV audience how he used to take angel dust and how much you helped him? Nancy Reagan listens real careful to every word China Sue says, and then looks her straight in the eye and says, Is that *all* you saw?

Yes, Mrs. Reagan, you were wonderful, oh, and then you said that this was only one of many young lives that had almost been ruined by the insanity of drugs. But tell me, dear, Nancy says, was it all in closeup? I don't know. Well, would anybody happen to have a needle? Nancy says. Tito's mouth drops open, my eyes bug out. And a little bit of thread? Nancy goes on. You see when the reporters left and I went into the ladies' room, I bent down to fix my hose and saw that the hem of my dress had come undone. In front.

And here we were supposed to go right on to a midnight supper to discuss the fund-raiser and I was stuck in the ladies' room with a sagging hem. So I went out another entrance hoping to find somebody who could help me fix the thing before I had to face another reporter. I was so terribly embarrassed, I just couldn't go back, and when I realized there wasn't anywhere to find a needle and thread this time of night, I panicked and began ringing doorbells and now I'm at wit's end . . .

She keeps going on like that while she parks her ass right at our kitchen table, and puts her purse down so I can take a good look at it. Genuine alligator. Well, I says to myself, too bad I didn't noticed that before, Nancy Reagan, when I was trying to figure was you shitting us.

So I go over to her, and real polite and everything says, You want a Bud? I'd love one, says Nancy. Well give her a glass, barks Tito. A glass will not be necessary, Nancy tells him.

Don't you worry, goes China Sue, I can fix that hem for you pronto. Tito, you got any thread? It'll have to be scarlet, says Nancy, or at least a magenta. She puts her hand to her ears to see if both earrings is still there and takes a swallow of beer.

Tito starts running all over the place, opening drawers, cursing, and slamming 'em shut, looking for thread. And I am wishing I'd cleaned up like he wanted me to before China Sue come over so's the place wouldn't look so bad.

Nancy Reagan takes a good look around, checks the place out. Well, look at you, I keep thinking. Here's the First Lady of our country, but she ain't wearing no diamonds or Gucci and not even one gold chain. Shit, if I had her money I'd be wearing ten gold chains and mink-lined Adidas.

So where are your parents this evening? she asks. Oh, they's out, I answer quick. Out to dinner. And will they be back soon? Nancy says, looking at the lipstick on her beer can and covering it up with her hand. Carlos ain't got no parents, Suzy pipes up. Everybody has parents, Nancy sasses back. So Suzy wraps the sheet over her head and ranks,

Well he don't, what you think a that? and Nancy stares up at the wall.

What about him, anyway? I says to my uncle, talking about my father. He dead or what? He ain't dead, he in jail, says Tito. You know that. And what does your father do? Nancy goes on, like Tito didn't say nothing. Construction, I tell her. But I lives with my uncle. Uncle here don't mind my staying here long's I clean up before he brings girls over. And I do all the laundry for the both of us too.

Well how about your little sister, says Nancy, can't she help out too? You mean Suzy? That ain't a sister. Can't you see she Chinese? She's Tito's wife. Carlos, shut your mouth! Suzy hollers, laughing. They ain't married and shit, I goes on, she's just his woman. And how old a woman *is* she? is Nancy's next dig. Fourteen, I says. But I'm eighteen. I got ID. You want to see it? I get up to get the proof I bought at Playland but Nancy starts waving me down.

Now don't you start giving me that kind of questioning shit in my own house, First Lady, Tito says, trying to sound polite. I wouldn't do it if I was in yours. Nancy pulls a mean face at him and grabs for the alligator purse, she opens it up. I'm really glad to have met all of you, she tells us in a sweet ho-voice. Did you find the thread? If I did I would a told you, says Tito, getting pissed. That's strange, she says in a voice gone all cold, that you don't have any, and she keeps looking through that purse. Come to think of it they said on television something about her having a gun in there.

Fiddlesticks! she says all of a sudden. Don't tell me I forgot that beeper? Now how am I ever going to get in touch with Jim? She snaps the purse shut loud and Suzy jumps and starts laughing again. The two of them acting so spooky, it's starting to scare the daylights out of me.

Who's this Jim? Tito'd like to know. We don't want no Jim up here. Jim's my bodyguard, and he's a perfectly lovely fellow, Nancy tells him. Yeah? You got a bodyguard? I says. She just gives me a look like don't put me on, dude. Shit, I goes on, I bet he gots some fresh weapons, I mean since you rule the country he can get his hands on just about anything. We don't rule the country, Nancy says, and starts looking bullets at me. Hold on a minute, I says to myself, and if she do got a gun in there? So I tell her how sorry I am about opening the door in my drawers. I really didn't know you was deciding to come and see us. And anyway, we got plenty of beer, why don't I put a little music on. That's sweet of you, she thanks me, and this time it's that same hooker's voice. Go ahead and do what you usually do.

So I put something mellow on. It's got a good beat. And before I know it I start relaxing and forget all about that we got the First Lady sitting right here. Tito and Suzy are maxing too. Come here, baby, he tells the Chi-nee. They snuggle up and bug out on each other, 'cause to tell the truth they was very high when they went to bed. Suzy got these problems in her pussy, she went to the hospital twice but they didn't do nothing. They said it was some kind of miscarriage and they sent her home stuffed up with Kotex but still bleeding. That was yesterday, I think, and since it hurt so much Tito give her all the crack she wants, he even put a little bit in her pussy. It was more than the hospital would do.

Finally I says, Nancy, you comfortable? I can call you that, right? Oh yes, she says, and I'm comfortable, but Ron must be worried. You mean the President, I says. No, she says, I mean Ron, Jr., my son. He was with me tonight. Then damn right, I agree with her. Like if I thought some drug addict at Odyssey House was to fuck with my mother or my sister I would be getting my gun already, they would not be alive today. You must care a lot about your mother and sister, she says. Yeah, I'm a family man. You want to see a picture of my baby girl? You mean a picture of your girlfriend? she says. No, I says, my little baby girl, she's a cute little thing. But weren't you just telling me about your girlfriends? says Nancy. I didn't tell you about no girlfriends, I says. Tito the only one brings girls up here, that why I got to clean the house up for him. I don't trust fooling around with no girls anymore. You never know who they been with. They all sick.

Sick? asks Nancy, and she starts playing with that hem again. Well, I says, I know this girl lost all her weight. They says she got the AIDS. Had these terrible headaches in the hospital. They wanted to cut her head open but she wouldn't let them. She left in the middle of the night 'cause they said they wouldn't let her out.

The First Lady lets go of that hem. The poor girl! she starts shouting at me. Yo, wait a minute, I tells her. I know rich people got delicate stomachs. But it ain't my fault. Me and my uncle are helping her out all the time. Anytime she wants to get high, we get her some dope 'cause we be willing to protect this dude that supplies it.

Oh, but this is terrible, terrible, says Nancy, like a little chick all of a sudden instead of an old lady. This is so terrible that I can't believe what you're saying is true. You are giving heroin to an AIDS victim. Well, yeah, I says, we are doing what we can because we are good people. We try to help out when we can. If I have my facts straight, she lays on me, drug abuse can give that awful disease to people. No shit, I says, you mean we're making her get more sick?

Just a minute, Tito interrupts, and he lets go of China Sue. Every time we get her high she thanks us and telling us how much better she is feeling. But that's only temporary, Nancy shoots back, you're killing her. We won't do it no more, Suzy promises. But the First Lady has already got a whole different look on her face, a bright idea. Write a letter to me, at the White House. A letter? says Tito. Well I ain't going to sign it. We're going to make certain this young girl gets help, says Nancy, that's all. You mean you got something that will make her feel better? I says. And she nods. It's all the lady will tell us and it sounds mysterious. Probably something only she can get hold of.

So I am worrying how am I going to write this letter when the worst thing happens. Because the doorbell starts to ring again. I keep making like it's not, but whoever it is is leaning on it like the First Lady did before. And the more it rings the madder Tito is getting. Until finally he starts calling out my name: Carlos, c'mere! And I go over and he shouts in my ear, Go downstairs and get rid of you-know-who!

That's when I realize I still got just my shorts on and run into the bedroom red as a beet. I start pulling on my pants quick so I can get down there and get rid of her before she gets inside the building—'cause I know who it be! But I know it's too late too, 'cause, someways, she is always getting in this building. I can hear those heels, then her calling through the door, Carlos, Carlos honey, open up!

Don't you answer that fucking door! Tito hisses at me, but she hears him and shouts back, What's a matter, you got a girl in there?

So Nancy grabs her purse quick and stands up. What's going on? she says loud, which is what we didn't need. All you ever do is lie to me! comes through the door, and Wait till I get my hands on you! Oh, says Nancy, even louder, Look at the trouble I'm causing after you were so nice. Young lady! Don't worry, I am not his girlfriend, I'm Nancy Reagan!

Bitch! comes the answer through the door, I'm Diana Ross! So Nancy gets right up and opens the door and says, You see? I'm not his girlfriend.

Well, it's this black queen comes up here sometimes. Calls herself Chaka Con, like the singer. She gives Nancy the onceover and can't believe her eyes. Honey, that drag is so convincing! But do you really want to look that old? Connie, shut up, says China Sue, this *is* the First Lady. Hmm, hmm, says Con, looks like the Last Lady to me.

Connie comes over to sit on my lap. Whatever got into me, thinking you was cheating on me. I take back everything I said.

Chaka, you got to leave, Tito tells her. I just finished saying to Carlos that he got to ask me first before he bring a drag queen up here. But instead of getting up, Connie gets mad. No queens, huh. Then what she doing here?

Connie, I tells her, this is Nancy Reagan for real. Ok, says Connie, it's a big world out there, and anybody can be anything they want. Nancy Reagan's got class and I can see somebody wanting to do her drag, if they can afford it. I ain't complaining. Now I'm black so I want to be Chaka or

Sheila E., but if I was white, I'd probably want to do Farrah Fawcett or somebody.

What you want here tonight? growls Tito. Ok, I'll get to the point. I come to get a ten but I only got five and I can bring the rest to you tomorrow. I don't sell that stuff no more, says Tito. What's a matter with you, says Connie, you know you can trust me. I really want to get high, baby. I'll make it worth you while. Both a you.

Chaka Con licks her lips and looks at Tito, then at me.

Me and Tito try to give the First Lady a look like what is this queen talking about, but Nancy has turned into some kind of statue. Maybe she has slipped a Valium. Chaka starts looking her up and down. What you doing here, honey? I ripped my dress, says Nancy. This isn't the girl you were telling me about, is it? Oh no, First Lady, I swears, this one don't take no dope.

Chaka Con takes in Nancy's purse. Oooh, look at that! It's just like the one Nancy was carrying on TV tonight. Where'd you get it and how you know she was gonna have it tonight? You come here to cop, girl? Why else would a white queen with an expensive purse come all the way down here? Come on, honey, share with your sisters, I'll give you five and you give me a rock.

So all of a sudden Nancy gets this look in her eyes like something dawned on her. No, that ain't it either, how can I explain it? It's like maybe that is happening somewhere in her head but then she deciding to show that to us. And slow like a statue with a motor in it she turns to me and says, *So that's what's going on.*

Tito hops up fast. After all this is the President's wife. You going to believe any nigger drag queen come in here out of the street, Mrs. Reagan? he says.

The Con hops up too. Wait a minute, dudes, what is going on here? I demand to know! Who is this queen and why is she making everybody so jumpy?

Chaka Con, says China Sue, I am trying to tell you! This is the First Lady! She come here to get her hem sewn.

So Chaka walks right up to the First Lady and looks into

her face. And then she takes a good look at the hands and the shoe size too, and says, Holy Shit, you're her! And she grabs hold the First Lady's hand, says, Mrs. Reagan, I didn't know, will you ever forgive me? I have admired you for such a long time. All my girlfriends love you.

It's perfectly all right, says the First Lady. I know you didn't know.

Chaka Con grabs a mirror out of her purse, checks herself out fast and throws it back in. Have you, have you known these folks long? she asks. We just met tonight, Nancy tells her. Umm, excuse me for asking, but in that purse, would you happen to have a needle and thread? No, honey, I mean Mrs. Reagan, I don't, says Connie like some kind of lady, I do all my sewing at home. In fact I am known as quite a seamstress. If you like, I will send my address to the White House and you can drop by for alterations anytime you please.

But Nancy gets a deep-freeze look in her eyes again, I never seen such a hard look, and gives a long sigh that everybody can hear, before she says, How kind of you to offer. Now who expected her to say that after that look and that sigh? But I need help now, she goes on, and drops her head and covers up her face with her hands. You can hear a pin drop.

Suzy is looking down at her feet, 'cause she don't want to see the First Lady that way. Me, I keep quiet. Finally Chaka says, Listen, now buck up, lady, c'mon now, I mean you are the First Lady, you ain't supposed to be crying like that over one silly little hem. Now cut it out, will you. You got responsibilities.

It's easy for you to say, Nancy whimpers, you don't know what it's like. Nobody does. So Chaka Con gets up and puts her hand on the First Lady's shoulder. Mrs. Reagan, Mrs. Reagan child, you stop that crying now. And the First Lady says, Well, we have feelings too.

Can I ask you something? Chaka says. You want me to get that needle and thread for you? Same color as the dress you're wearing? That would be ever so kind of you, the First Lady mumbles through her fingers.

Then don't you worry, Mrs. Reagan, croons Connie, but—uh, well there ain't no stores open now, oh I mean I could get you some black thread—the First Lady shivers a little when she says this to her—but to match your color, well I'm going to have to go all the way up to 128th Street, to a friend's a mine . . .

Nancy looks up. Then you'd better hurry. Do you need cab fare? Well, the cab costs a lot, I hate to ask you for that, child, says Chaka Con. But already Nancy is opening that purse and all of us kind of leaning over to peek inside.

How much do you need? says Nancy.

How much do I need? How much do I need? says Chaka. Mrs. Reagan, I got lots of needs. See this wig? See these shoes, see this dress? Well, the wig costs money, the shoes costs money, and the dress costs money. You know how it is, don't you. I been looking for a job. I sure hope I find one tomorrow. Because, you know, I'm not like those other niggers out there. How I look, the kind of image I have, well, that's important to me. I can't stand people don't take care a themselves. People who let themselves go and ain't got no respect for themselves. They make me sick, you know what I mean? They lying in their own shit, they expect other people to carry the load for them and then's they don't appreciate it when's they do! And I don't want to be one of those people. I mean it's hard for all of us, ain't it? All I need is just a little headstart, things is bad now but all I need is just a little push to get me going 'cause I got plans. And once I get going nothing can stop me. What you got in that purse there, anyways?

Nancy shuts that purse fast. You—you got a weapon in there? Connie says, and she looks up at Tito and swallows. Don't believe everything you read in the papers, Nancy sneers. I didn't mean nothing by that, Mrs. Reagan. Now listen, you want me to get that needle and thread for you?

The First Lady's eyes kind of go dim. I suppose so, she says. Well, gimme a hundred dollars, says Con.

Nancy starts to freeze up again but makes a big effort. She looks real hard at Chaka Con and she starts to blink a

whole lot. I pay it back to you, says Chaka. So Nancy goes
back in that purse and takes out two fifty-dollar bills, hands
'em to the Con. Tito, Chaka says, can I talk to you for a
minute? But what about the thread? Nancy says. Oh I'm
going right out, child, lickety-split.

Chaka gets up and gallops into the bathroom.

So now me and Suzy are sitting there alone with the First
Lady, and Suzy is just looking down at her feet and finally
says, I got to get a drink of water, and trots away too. And
I'm left there staring at Nancy so after a minute I says
excuse me too and go in the bathroom too. And Tito is just
now lighting up that pipe and Chaka Con got it stuck between her lips. But when she sees all these folks and only
one little rock in there, she says, C'mon, load it up, I want a
king-size toke.

So we begin to get high, and 'cause Tito has really packed
that pipe up, after two tokes my head is rushing like you
wouldn't believe. So when we hear Nancy banging on that
door, we look at each other and bursts out laughing. But
finally Tito says, Well we got to go out there. And ones of
us got to go find that thread for her. And that'll be you,
right, Chaka Con? And Connie looks at him and says, Unh,
unh, baby. I'm the one got us this money to pay for all this
shit, I ain't going nowhere. So Tito says, Carlos, you got to
go and find that thread. And I tell him, I'm too stoned. So
we decide that we going to tell her that Chaka just remembered that friend she thought she had on 128th Street ain't
there no more, she made a big mistake. And if she asks us
for the money back, we only give her twenty because she
owes us the rest for letting her chill out here. 'Cause wouldn't
the kind of hotel that she would go to cost even more?

So we go out there together and tell the First Lady just
how it has to be. And everybody is waiting for her to get
shit-faced mad and call that bodyguard to come back here.
You can imagine how surprised we are then when Nancy
don't get mad at all. She just sits there, with that alligator
purse in her skinny lap and her knobby hands folded on top
of it. Life has its slaps in the face, she says, I'd be the first to

admit that. So Tito tells her no hard feelings but some folks don't find it so easy to get by. And Nancy answers him back, I've seen more than you can probably imagine. And Suzy says to her, But First Lady, I thought you was living in some kind of wonder dream. And Nancy Reagan looks her straight in the eye and says, Well, the dream I am living, that fairy-tale dream that I wake up to each morning, in which I am lying next to the kindest, bravest, and most understanding—and I suppose the most powerful—man in the world, well that dream came true for me but I had to work for it. Lord knows I worked to make that dream come true. And looking around me at you, I see these bright, young shining faces. Sure they have suffered a lot already, but they still are alive and burning and aching with the desire to have the things they should have.

And then she says, Do you know what? I've got a funny feeling. Call it an intuition, but you and you and you and you, you'll have that dream someday. And that's why it is such a joy to look into your eager young eyes and see the power to make it happen . . .

Well, I didn't hear the rest of what Mrs. Reagan was saying, 'cause suddenly my head started to float. It was like—well it was like we are always going to movies me and Tito and my friends. It's all we ever do side from getting high. Now here comes the part where the basketball player kid who up to now is the underdog meets some older person making him realize that he can make it too. It's the part we all like the best, but we never knew nobody who was going to do that in real life. I mean somebody who could really say that to us. So it was a great high. And suddenly that nervous skinny old lady sitting there got changed into some kind of holy lady. Or a queen. Yeah, that's it, a queen holding out this wand, and each time she points it at somebody everything goes all right. You gonna be rich now. Or maybe that's not it. But it is like you going to be rich and have everything you want.

But the most bugged-out thing of all, that's when I look over and see Connie and she's crying. I can hardly hear her but she is saying that, O, Nancy, you came to visit us and we done treated you horrible, girl, we showed you no respect, you know what I be doing with that money you gave me already, I—

Hush! says Nancy. There is no need. I don't need the thread any more because the experience I have had here is a million times more fulfilling than any press conference or TV camera. I will go back to Odyssey House and tell them about this experience. Nancy stands up and it's like a ray of sun shining on us, and she says, Would you mind if I used your bathroom?

So Nancy gets up and goes to the bathroom. And we keep sitting there saying nothing. I look at Tito, and China Sue, and Chaka Con, and I see changed people. Nobody can talk.

Then we start to hear it. I guess I was the first one. Plop plop plop. And I realize I can hear the First Lady. And Tito looks up and so does Chaka Con and China Sue, and we look into each other's eyes, and finally I says it, because I know that's what we all thinking. Wouldn't it be fresh if we could get a look at the First Lady taking a dump?

So one by one we all get up and tiptoe toward the bathroom door to peer through the crack, to watch the First Lady drop her load. She's got her dress all bunched up and held out in front of her, and the panty hose are just kind of shoved down at her ankles. I don't know but I expected the First Lady to roll them panty hose down. And then she reaches for the paper—and if you thought about it—well wouldn't the First Lady take just a few squares at a time and put them on top of each other all neat so that the edges matched? Well this one just grabbed the end of the roll and yanked. But then something else happened, and I don't know if I want to tell you about it. But ok, I will, and what happened then was, instead of lifting the edge of her ass off the seat and wiping, the First Lady stood up. And when she did, it knocked us all on our ass, because the biggest cock you've ever seen flipped out the top those panty hose.

Well at first it was like a punch in the gut. I mean, being

stoned and all, we couldn't get over it—that the First Lady wasn't no lady. But finally Chaka Con gets enough breath and says, Child, child, child, you mothafucka, you pulled the wool over our eyes. And the First Lady yanked up the panty hose and pulled off her wig and came out laughing, big, loud, low laughs, laughs I heard before. And Tito, who can hardly get his breath neither, manages to cuff me on the head, gasping, You fool, didn't I tell you it was a drag queen. And then still laughing, everybody goes to punch Brand X, 'cause that's who it was. This drag queen Brenda from the Deuce. They call her Brenda X or Brand X most the time. And Tito still gasping, I knew it all along, and Brand X laughing and laughing and saying, Like hell you did, and going to grab that crack pipe, saying, Give me that shit, 'cause I am the one who paid for it. And Suzy laughing and saying, No you wasn't, it was Nancy Reagan. And where'd you get that kind of money, girl, Chaka Con is saying. You wouldn't believe the sick trick from Washington, says Brand X, gave me five hundred to put on this drag so he could pretend he was fucking Nancy Reagan. And then the pipe starts going around and our heads fill up with smoke and the First Lady shrinks away, right back to TV size.

A Visit from Mom

Last night, when I had sex with a suspected murderer. It was in the Carter Hotel, or maybe the Rio or the Fulton. About six this morning, actually.

Was it in the Carter, or was it the Fulton? I forget which one. It's the one that lets you pay with a credit card. After which you must convince the second party to leave when you do. Or else the signed credit slip at the desk will have the time added to it until he decides to check out. This is a situation that might be called awkward—isn't it?—when the second party is homeless and when, if you stay, you won't get any sleep yourself . . . no . . . you probably wouldn't.

I had come from Port Authority where I had taken Mom to make sure she got on the airport bus safely. I wanted to make certain. There are a lot of troublemakers hanging around Port Authority. Mom was in New York for a regional conference of the United Jewish Appeal. Since her conference was near the Algonquin, I had told her to meet me there for a drink. From there I knew it would be easy to get a cab to Port Authority, a few blocks away. Mom is beginning to have a little trouble getting around, and the streets were icy.

Everyone knows Port Authority is an unofficial shelter for the homeless. The terminal is not far from the *Times* building on Forty-third Street, opposite which is a place where drag queens wearing gowns and pants suits go to use the bathroom or perfume themselves at the bar. But today, as it was barely six P.M., only a poor queen named Missy was sitting at the bar. Missy was dressed down in a muddy old

16

turtleneck. The bar was stifling, but I kept my coat on. It was the one I'd bought on sale at Barney's that I knew Mom would approve of. I was also wearing the sweater that she had sent me for Hanukkah.

I remember thinking how pretty Mom still looks with her soft white hair, sparkling blue eyes, and lots of rouge. Yet what a relief it is to get her safely onto the airport bus and know that she's on her way home. I guess it's a relief, although after she's gone, I always miss seeing her. Over sherry and peanuts, Mom had told me about her work with the less fortunate aged, the Meals on Wheels program she helps organize in our hometown, the parties for senior citizens, the craft afternoons at the center. Mom had also been to Lord & Taylor that day to look for knitwear for Aunt Heidi. I chided her for sallying out over the icy sidewalks, but I didn't make a big deal out of it, because I figure Mom's sense of independence is the most important thing she has left.

I must have been in the bar at least an hour when the bouncer came in with his brother. The brother looked like he had been in jail. He had a jail body. It's a thickness of certain parts coming from constant, unsupervised exercise of those parts, I suppose. Nor was his goatee, or the tattoos that said AVENGER and BABY LOVE, any evidence to the contrary, especially since the tattoos looked like they'd been drawn with a razor blade, after which shoe polish is carefully rubbed in the wound. The bouncer took his seat by the door, while his brother went to sit on a stool by the bathroom. It was the brother's job to keep an eye on the head.

Mom is having a little trouble getting around these days. I guess it's osteoporosis. But otherwise she is clear as a bell and just as energetic as ever. She and I have always been as close as anyone could be. Whenever I had a secret, an adolescent worry about not being popular or sports-minded enough—when I thought I would die if I didn't tell somebody —there was Mom, eager to lend an ear. I always told her. And I still do, almost always. Yet there are now certain things I just would not say to Mom, because I figure that

being close to the end—her own mortality—is enough for
her to worry about. It's time I took care of my problems
myself.

Yet by the second sherry, Mom's irrepressible concern
rose to the surface. She said that she had had enough of
talking about herself and wanted to know all about what
was going on in my life. What about the job in school
production at the textbook company? Was I happy there
and did I think there was some kind of future?

Although I myself have never been in prison, I feel that
my great sociability, cheerful openness, and keen, observant
behavior have informed me about the experience. Having
been in jail must be, I've always thought, a powerful psychic
marker. I will admit that there is something about a person
who has been in jail that attracts me. Which is not to say I
take the experience at all lightly—I doubt that I would
survive it. But how does someone who has been in jail
speak to his wife or child when he is pleased or displeased
by her or his behavior? How does somebody who has been
in jail make love with somebody else? What would he be
thinking about to get excited? Having been in prison leaves
its imprint on a person's body, which becomes vigilant and
tense like a coil. Yet a person who has been in jail seems
somewhat resigned; his body speaks of great patience. Take
the bouncer's brother, with his strong-looking wrists, stubby,
scarred hands, sullen face, and tattoos reading ON THE EDGE,
AVENGER, etc., running up one bulging arm. As he perched
on the stool, he held a wooden club, one eye constantly on
the bathroom door, though there was still no one in the bar
except myself and Missy. No, he could wait all night for
somebody to try to use the bathroom for the wrong purpose, the hand was waiting on the club.

Exactly what did I do between this time and six in the
morning? What could I have been doing in all that time? I
keep wondering. I put Mom on the bus for her plane, which
was supposed to leave at eight-thirty . . . so I must have put
her on the bus near seven; I must have sat with her in Port
Authority until a little after seven. Which means I didn't get

to the bar until after seven. I guess it is a relief that she's gone, though I do kind of miss her. But there are so many things that could happen to her in this dangerous city. Also, I start to resent her prying too much into my business. I now remember that as we sat waiting for the bus, she brought up the job business again. She said she knew from experience, from the days when she and Dad were both working to make enough money to give the children a nice home and a good education, that by a certain age—my age, she added pointedly, looking at me with her piercing, uncompromising blue eyes—a person has to make a real commitment to a job, instead of just camping out there, if he wants to get somewhere.

I decided that there was no sense in complaining to Mom about the job. No sense in trying to explain that mechanically shifting papers from one desk to another, keeping logs and making lists, writing memos, was far from anything a real human could make a commitment to. I didn't want Mom to know that I hated working there, even felt humiliated by it sometimes. What sense would it have made to tell her that? To make her worry about my future as she sat in the dismal departures area of Newark airport waiting for a plane that would take her back to desolate upstate? So all I said was that the job was just a way of making money. Clear and simple. I didn't like it or dislike it and that was good enough for me.

Now I remember. I didn't stay in the bar the whole time. Instead I left to go eat—hadn't the bartender said it was nine-thirty shortly before?—across the street to get some lamb from the Greek. It was surprisingly good lamb, and I ate a very gelatinous rice pudding. As I ate, through the window I could see a few queens making their way across the ice to the bar. Their heels looked so skinny and high that I was afraid one of them would slip and fall. It was so cold out, but even so, a lot of them were dressed to the nines. Why not go back to the bar? I thought.

Why not go back to the bar?

As we sat in Port Authority, the conversation had somehow turned to Mom's will and her worries that I would not handle the money she had "slaved for" in any reasonable way. It is my opinion that Mom should really think about enjoying the money herself while she still can. Instead of worrying about how I am going to use it. In the first place, she has nothing to worry about, and in the next place, if she wants to put restrictions on it from beyond the grave, then she shouldn't be leaving her precious money to me at all.

"Who knows? Your father and I could use it all up in a nursing home if we got sick," Mom suggested.

Seeing the queens slide across the ice to the bar had made me want to go back in. If Mom wanted to put restrictions on me from beyond the grave, that was fine, but tonight I didn't want to think about it. Inside the bar I recognized another queen, a very tall Latin in a leopard-print sheath, pantomiming the song that was playing to a tubby business-man. Missy was propped in a corner. Her face looked anesthetized into a Mona Lisa smile. The very strong wrists of the bouncer's brother were still resting on the club in his lap as he sat perched near the head. It was as if the wrists were on display; I remember that I kept looking at them. Finally I spoke to him. "What's up?"

"I'm working, man," he answered.

The bouncer's brother started to talk. He was from the Bronx, but he was trying to get a place to stay in Manhat-tan. And yes, he had been in jail, a year and a half, or maybe six months, ago—but it was a strange story that he guessed most people wouldn't believe. It seems that he had been arrested on suspicion of killing his twin brother. They had been smoking crack all day (something he used to do but didn't do anymore, he added)—and when one of the "rocks" from one of the vials seemed to have disappeared, he began thinking that his twin was holding out on him, after which he started to turn the room upside down. (In fact, it had happened at the Carter, or was it the Fulton?) He turned over the mattress and looked under tables, crawled on his hands and knees across the carpet looking for the rock, until he was overcome with anger at his twin, whom he thought he had caught a glimpse of in the mirror laughing at him; so he went to his brother's clothes—both of them were naked at the time because it was summer and there was no air-conditioning—he went to the clothes and looked in all the pockets, he even tore the cuffs of the pants apart, but still didn't find the rock, so he decided to send his brother out to get more. Neither of them had any money. "That don't matter to me," he growled, feeling as if he were about to snap, "You go out there and you find another bottle 'cause you been holding out on me." And since he was four minutes older than his brother, the brother obeyed.

The rest is somewhat unclear, but the gist of it seems to be that his twin happened to go to a bodega on Ninth Avenue looking for crack just when there was a drug war going on; supposedly mistaken for a backup man, he was shot. After which somebody—who is now in hiding, but at the time was staying in a room next door at the hotel—testified that he had heard the twins arguing shortly before the murder . . .

I feel really bad about the way Mom said good-bye. With the talk about the will the last topic we spoke of. I didn't want Mom to know how much I hated that job, or that I was planning on leaving it. So I held it in. Mom must have been out for blood, though, because the more I would try to shift the subject to something uncontroversial, the more adamantly she returned to what she surmised might be my problems. Then suddenly she said, "You drink too much."

To be perfectly honest, I had been to an AA meeting just the night before. I have never had a blackout or hurt myself or anything like that, but I was worried about the amount of time I was wasting getting drunk. The AA meeting only seemed to increase my anxiety. Their never fully acknowledged portrayal of drinking as a world entered by excess, a world that was ruled tyrannically by drink, in which you could never hope for any control except by self-exile; the idea that you had to go through a door to another world that was just as uncontrollable as the first, but that was more conventional, and structured in a way that made your survival more likely; the idea that you had to endure life knowing that this door between the two worlds was always there, yet never opening it again . . . seemed to transform living into a continual struggle against the temptation for self-annihilation.

I wanted to live as if there were one world, not two.

It was time for Mom to get on the bus. I assured her that I wasn't drinking too much, but this did not seem to allay her fears entirely. Instead she began to talk about diaper days. There was a startling contrast between me and my older brother, she said, who had suffered greatly because of hyperactivity and its effect on the nerves of others, while I had been a practically troubleless toddler who never complained and always smiled and laughed, who spoke in complete sentences by the age of one and a half; these sentences often incorporated the word *please*. But then, by adolescence, the two brothers seemed mysteriously to change places: The older brother abruptly settles down and starts doing what he is supposed to. He enters medical school. Now the younger brother begins ". . . sowing wild oats. I guess your brother had already gotten it out of his system."

I actually didn't go to the bar right after I left Port Authority. It occurs to me that I went to the peep show at Show World. There was a film in my booth called *Bigger the Better* with a scene in a classroom in which the teacher asks one student to stay after class because his marks are not up to par. They end up making it, during which the student, who has an inhumanly large cock, fucks the teacher in the ass on top of a desk.

As I kissed Mom good-bye at the bus, I took a good look at what she was wearing. She was wearing a lovely suit of pink wool, and her shoes were cream, very fashionable. Mom refused to wear "old-lady" shoes even if they might be more practical at this point. She was holding a cream-colored purse and her suede briefcase that I assumed was full of papers having to do with the United Jewish Appeal. "Take care of yourself, honey," she said.

It wasn't the strenuousness of Mom's occasional visits to

New York that worried me, but her life-style in the wintry land of upstate New York with my aging father. Both of them still drove despite his considerable loss of eyesight and her hearing problem. Her reflexes were obviously much slower than they had been in her prime, and although the area was far from congested, compared to this city, I was constantly picturing the sudden swerve of a car at a lonely intersection, literally feeling the brittle fragility of their old bones at the impact of the accident. What, the thought had sometimes occurred to me, despite my efforts to repress it, would I do if one of them were injured and totally incapacitated, yet lingered for years? How would I manage to care for them? How much, I thought with a guilty swallow, was I depending on the security of my inheritance? Anyway, neither of them understood or approved of what they thought of as my life-style. Something told me that any inheritance would have severe restrictions placed on it in an effort to control my life—after their death—according to a plan of their choosing.

During the recitation of the bouncer's brother, who had been arrested for the murder of his twin brother, his broad wrists stayed displayed on the club, unmoving. He told me that, in actuality, he was working two jobs this evening. He had to watch the bathroom to keep the crack-heads from going in and to keep the drag queens from turning tricks in there. But if I was looking for a good time, he would be glad to get somebody else to take over for him. I went into the john and counted the bills in my pocket, realizing that—not counting whatever might be in the envelope Mom had slipped into my hand as her lips brushed mine before stepping onto the bus—I had only thirty dollars. Taking Mom's envelope out of my pocket, I opened it, glancing at the front of the card on which were written the words *To My Son*. Inside it was fifty dollars. The bouncer's brother had said he wanted sixty, and I was planning to use my credit card for the hotel room. I left the bathroom and nodded to the bouncer's brother, who went to speak to the bartender.

The bouncer's brother is called Mike. I was disturbed by

the fact that Mike left the bar wearing only his T-shirt. "I'll pick up my coat in a minute," he assured me cryptically. Then, as soon as I had paid for the room, he took a long, mumbling look at the number on the key and handed it back to me. "Wait for me up there and I'll be back."

How, I wondered, as I stood in the room still wearing my coat, had I ended up waiting on the fourteenth floor of a hotel—it was the Rio, I think—for someone who had been accused of murdering his brother? The setup was beginning to seem more and more obvious to me. He knew the room number. After he went back, supposedly to get his coat, he would return with a friend, who would wait somewhere on this floor. At the right moment, perhaps with the aid of a weapon to keep me still, Mike would leap up and let his friend in. The two of them would roll me.

Mom and Dad's golden, or fiftieth, anniversary a couple of years ago was our most successful family affair in years. My brother Joe and I had planned it, though it had begun as his idea. For our celebration, we chose an inn by the lake where the whole family had spent countless summers when we were children. "Don't get us anything extravagant," Mom had cautioned. "We won't live long enough to enjoy it." Joe and I hadn't listened. Together we bought Mom a gold watchband and Dad a high-tech snowblower for the driveway. Unfortunately, I had been short of money at the time and had to work out an agreement with Joe where I paid for only a quarter of it. Dinner at the inn had taken on the form of a joyous tribute to the longevity of my parents' relationship. And all of Mom's and Dad's oldest friends were there. Our cousins even came all the way from California. It occurred to me that Mom and Dad had always acted on their concern for me by being intensely practical on my birthdays, Bar Mitzvah, and graduation, never getting me anything that was likely to be damaged by childish carelessness —no matter how much I begged for it.

There was a knock on the door of the hotel room, but I stood rooted. Finally Mike began calling me through a crack in the door. "Hey, will you open up, it's me."

Trembling, I moved to the door and opened it slightly. Mike pushed it against me so that I stumbled backwards, and he walked in. Then he closed the door and locked it.

"What's a matter with you?" he asked, staring at my still-coated figure. "You hiding a gun there or something?"

Mike started to undress until he was down to his underwear. His body was an unstable column of muscles beginning at his shoulders and lats and tapering only at his shins and feet. One nipple was sliced diagonally by a six-inch scar. The name Mickey had been hand-tattooed above his waist. "Well, go ahead," he said. "Peel down."

Only because I noticed that Mike placed all of his clothes on a table, out of reach of the bed, did I hesitantly begin to remove my coat. For I knew that if he had been hiding a weapon, he would have kept the clothes within reach of the bed. I took off my shoes. Mike, in his black briefs, stood watching. Was I imagining that one ear seemed to be cocked toward the door?

Mike got onto the bed and motioned me to him. In my white briefs, I padded to the edge of the bed and sat down. "Relax, man, would you," he muttered. I lay down next to him and he raised one hand and tweaked my nipple. Then he said, "This may have to cost you."

In fact, the aforementioned lake at which our family had summered often returned in dreams. For my birthday, which is in July, Mom would bake the kind of layered butter-frosting cake you rarely see anymore, and Dad would make hot dogs and hamburgers on the grill. Aunt Heidi always came out for the day on Greyhound, and in her bag was a present for me. Two rules were waived for the day: I was allowed to take the boat as far away as I wanted, and I could stay up as long as I liked. Understandably, my memories of those days have the scent of adventure, sun-spangled water followed by endless nights shot with stars.

"Relax, man, would you. I mean, you got to pay more depending on what you want to do." Mike leapt to a standing position on the bed and pulled down the black briefs. With his back to me, and legs straddling mine, he bent forward and spread his cheeks. "How's this? Look at that hole. Isn't it something?" He began to gyrate.

As soon as I had slipped on the rubber that I got out of my wallet, Mike began to twist his ass onto my cock. He straddled me and began to rock back and forth so that the bed shook and my cock slid in and out. Clenching his teeth, he mumbled, "That's right, man, it belongs to you. Treat it right and you'll own it." Then, having soon been directed to "shoot that cream deep inside," I hastened toward an orgasm, after which Mike raised himself deftly from my phallus.

"I'm hungry," Mike said.

"What's this you said about it costing me?"

Mike's body stiffened as his eyes got that look of someone about to begin a complicated tale. "You don't know who you're with," he began. "You don't know who you've got right here in this room." Mike went on to detail his identity. According to him, he was closely connected to the bar owners—too closely for comfort, he added. As a matter of fact, one of them, after whom the bar took its name, had been watching our every move and had instructed Mike to leave his jacket as collateral before we walked together to the hotel. Mike had been very hesitant to go with me at all, "seeing that these guys tend to think they own somebody and I am kind of their boy." But they had generously given their permission. Go with the guy and give him a good time, they had counseled when he came back for the coat. But make sure he makes it worth your while. Now what would Mike do, he wanted me to tell him, if he came back to the bar with his ass full of grease and didn't have all the money— the one hundred and fifty dollars—they were expecting? What is more, it would be foolish for me to suppose that they couldn't find out where anybody lived.

Dipping my hand into my pants pocket, I pulled out all the cash I had. Mom's card flipped out, too, and floated down to the floor. "Hey!" Mike said, bending toward the card, "is it your birthday?"

I knelt quickly and snatched the card away, bending it in half as I stuffed it back in my pocket.

"Don't touch that!" I snapped.

Mike and I began to get dressed, but he was stewing. "There's only eighty dollars here," he hissed. "What the fuck do you expect me to say when I get back?"

"I told you, that's all I have."

But Mike was not to be daunted. Crawling around the carpet, he began cursing, accusing me of taking his socks. When he stood up, his face was livid and his entire muscular body was trembling. "All right, keep the damn socks," he spat, "if you're that kind of pervert, but you gotta pay for 'em!" He pulled his Adidases on over bare feet, grabbed me roughly by the Hanukkah sweater, and forced me toward the door. "C'mon, man, you must have a bankcard in that wallet. We're going to a cash machine!" As we left the room, I noticed dirty white socks sticking out from under the bed.

Planes move so incredibly faster than real time, and by now, six A.M., Mom would have gotten home long ago and been asleep, with Dad, her husband, for several hours. I do hope she got home safely and that there was no trouble at the airport.

Family Romance

"Take that stuff again and you have a good chance of dying in the process, clear and simple," he said. He put my chart back in the folder. That's all there was to say. An irregularity had been found in my EKG, due, the doctor suspected, to cocaine. Cocaine having been taken in the most powerful way possible: inhaled in a gaseous state, reaching the cells of the brain in less than ten seconds, causing an almost instantaneous jump in blood pressure. One muscle of the heart had been overexercised, and that put pressure on the other parts, as I understood it. My heart wasn't normal.

I was in our wood-paneled den watching the news, listening to a report about an athlete who had probably died from an overdose. It seems his wife had called an ambulance when he started going into convulsions. By the time they got him to the hospital, it was too late. If it hadn't been for this news, I probably would not have been thinking at that moment of the doctor's visit. Especially since I wasn't alone. My adopted son was sitting on the bed, puffing on a cigarette; my wife standing in the door frame, hand on hip.

We'd just finished a painful conversation about my son moving back in here, and he was against the idea. My wife was for it and was using money as a pivotal issue. But my son maintained that since he is eighteen, the decision should be entirely up to him. What's more, he hadn't lived in this house for four years. His leaving had been my wife's idea, not mine. But it also had been my wife's idea to adopt a child.

We'd been trying to have a baby for almost six years

28

when we adopted him. We'd been through everything available at the time, including a doubtful surgical procedure, but nothing worked. Then came adoption agencies with decade-long waiting lists. So we put an advertisement in the *Pennysaver*. It was composed by my wife and went something like this:

> Couple with love to spare
> would like to share it with a
> healthy white baby.
> Generous reward.
> We are a stable family.

I argued that the word *white* was too blatantly racist. We'd just wait and see when we met the people, I suggested. Then we could always say yes or no. But my wife was adamant that the word stay in. As her trim hands sliced carrots and celery for a roast, she passionately began defending the word *white*, claiming that the baby had to resemble as much as possible something that could have come from her. She had to feel, in fact, that it was hers. This would be the only compensation for our inability to make ourselves live on through succeeding generations. Our failure was made even worse, she contended, flinging the roast abruptly into the oven, by the fact that she was an only child, the end of her line.

I gave in. And late one night we had our first response. He was a man on the telephone known only as Sloane. He knew where he could get us a white baby, if we wanted one. But a white one would cost a lot. Was he the father of the baby? I asked. The idea must have seemed absurd to him, as he scoffed, far from it. Then he designated a place on the highway about a mile from a shopping mall in another suburb where we were to meet him if we were really interested.

My wife was at the mirror, yanking her short reddish hair into a ponytail. Her eyes welled with desperation when I protested the wisdom of dealing with such a character as Sloane. My hesitation made her furious. Why was she being put in such a position, she demanded to know, when all she wanted was an ordinary baby? There was nothing unusual about her ambition. Women a hundred times more unremarkable than herself were granted the wish without the slightest hesitation. Why should she be denied? She made up her mind to meet Sloane whether I went with her or not, slipped into duck shoes (it was raining), and stormed out to the Honda.

She careened into the driveway about an hour later, her pert face pale and fervent, her eyes burning. It was all settled. They'd agreed on a price. She'd given him a check already. Apprehensively I questioned her about Sloane but could discover little. Of course I'd been right, she said haltingly. He was probably a very dangerous man. Those eyes, those eyes, she kept repeating. As for his sources for adoption, they had to be criminal. It would be best to have as little to do with him as possible. Just get it over with fast. The child would be delivered the very next evening.

That night in bed, she pulled me toward her. To be honest, she didn't have much information about our child, she whispered in my ear. Only that it was guaranteed white and healthy. The necessary papers would be delivered with it too.

Her precipitous determination was fate, like a pregnancy. It was like something happening inside one for which two had to share the responsibility. Strangely enough, over the misgivings, the news that I was about to become a father made me feel proud, almost powerful.

We spent the whole of the next day driving to outlets that sold strollers and playpens. My wife said that we were going to have a boy. We furnished the guest room in our ranch-style house with a crib, blue polka-dot curtains, and some toys.

It was midnight, and still no one had come. Are you sure you gave him the right address? I asked my wife timidly.

One would think so, was the curt reply. Then she grimly
began to change into her nightgown.

We were awakened by the crunch of car tires on gravel in
the driveway, followed by a heavy thud. Headlights flooded
the window as a car screeched away. My wife and I ran out
in our nightclothes to see what looked like a bag of laundry
lying on the lawn near the rosebushes. The bag was moving.
When I untied it, a boy of about eight crawled out.

My wife brought him into the house and began to exam-
ine him. She clasped his forehead to her breast to see if he
had a fever and checked his teeth. His hair was matted and
his nails looked dirty, so she led him to the tub.

I stood in the doorway to the bathroom, watching the
soapy washcloth slide over his soft-looking body. He didn't
look exactly white, more likely Hispanic, as he was somewhat coffee-colored. He had large, liquid black eyes, a full,
slightly drooling mouth, and a flat nose.

It's not a baby, I pointed out, not daring to mention the
race thing as well. He needs a mommy and daddy, my wife
retorted.

Of course, the crib, the stroller, and the playpen had to
be gotten rid of. We bought a bed for him. My wife spent a
large part of the next year sleeping near or on it. It was
because of what had happened to him in the past. He was
afraid to be alone at night, she said.

What first struck me about my adopted son was that he
didn't seem to know very many words. If he had a native
language other than English, I never discovered what it was.
"Mine," he would say with a frown, grabbing a piece of
steak right off the fork at the barbecue, then dropping it in
the grass with a howl because it was too hot. Or he would sit
with his back to me in front of the television, barking over
and over, "Change! Change!" until I got up and flipped the
dial.

My wife pieced together a story for him. It was gleaned
from their nights together and from the books on child
abuse that she had begun to lap up. He was likely to have
come from a Central or South American country where he'd

led a wretched existence as a throwaway, she said. To survive, he may have resorted to stealing or worse practices. He could have spent his day wading through industrial dumps in search of machine parts to sell on the street. Such dumps were known to contain caustic chemicals, which could explain the strange discolorations—perfectly even reddish bands, like slave bracelets—around each of his ankles.

It was clear that he would require special patience and attention. We talked about his need to feel loved, accepted. But there was something about him. He didn't really seem like a kid. I felt it, for example, when I snapped his picture as he hung from a jungle gym or put on a pom-pom-festooned hat at a birthday party. I could see him—unlike other kids his age—turning to get a good angle, coming on to the camera.

What is more, having a child hadn't strengthened our marriage at all. It was as if my wife were in a trance whose circle was closed to me. Motherhood for her was a bliss bordering on the manic. Things that had bothered her before couldn't touch her now. The child was more important.

When I suggested to my wife that her absorption in our son was unhealthy, obsessive, she countered by accusing me of a lack of sensitivity for the boy that was based on a character disorder. I was borderline, she said. I had never really felt anything. I was cold and I always withdrew from everybody. As an example, she cited our sex life. What had before been passionate, involved sex, spiced by a desperate desire to create human life (before time ran out), had become routine and faceless. I'd stopped taking the challenge. There was no more commitment on my part, only a dull desire to get off. And how could I disagree? I'd sunk into a kind of apathy that I don't really think of as my life anymore.

My waistline sagged and I was getting out of breath on stairs. I had no real friends. My work wasn't going well at all. I'd gone free-lance to give myself a more flexible schedule, with the excuse that I'd be able to spend more quality time at home. But I did nothing with the extra time. I became a fanatic sports spectator, bellowing with rage if

anyone dared to place a hand on the dial. I felt regarded as
no more than a fixture in my own home, an out-of-date
piece of furniture gathering dust in front of the television.
And my son was already thirteen.

He looked different. Maybe it was his hairstyle, identical
to boys' his age in the neighborhood, that made him look
more Caucasian; still, I could have sworn that his skin
looked less brown, his nose and lips less blunt. His English
was casual and colloquial now. It sounded fake, as far as I
was concerned. I couldn't shake the feeling that he was
playing at being average. For example, he made a point of
pretending an utter lack of anxiety about the future. "We'll
just handle that one when it comes around" was one of his
bland remarks, ostensibly put forth to soothe too-neurotic
me when I expressed a worry that couldn't have been all
that unreasonable. Then he'd go out to play hockey. I'd sit
home and watch hockey on television, pop open another
can of beer. Or maybe he'd gone to the science club or the
debate team or the karate studio.

My wife had hung awards and trophies for these activities
on the wood paneling of the den, where I sat in front of the
TV set. There was a plaque with a big, gold-painted plastic
test tube. He'd gotten it for being third runner-up at a
science fair. Then there was a laminated report card for a
semester in which he had scored a B+ average, and a
framed photo of him smashing a board with his foot at a
junior-level karate exhibition. Surrounding me at various
points in the room were other paraphernalia: a computer
that had a chess program, an Andre the Giant wrestling
video, a Yamaha electric piano, and a punching bag on a
wire pole.

His own room was his own world. There was a camouflage-
print tent pitched over the bed, a can of sterno on the
dresser, next to an empty, encrusted cage once inhabited by
a now defunct iguana. Interspersed with rock posters and
bicycle parts were implements for survival in the jungle: a
hide skinner, some snakebite suction cups, and an army-
green compass.

One day while he was at school, my eyes were drawn to the corner of a yellow envelope sticking from his top dresser drawer. For some reason I took it out and opened it. It was stuffed with scraps of paper torn from a loose-leaf notebook, a kind of scrawled diary.

"Saw Sloane again today. So cool. He had on fatigues."

"Sloane got his nipple pierced today."

"Did crack with Sloane again. Bare-assed."

From the bottom of the envelope tumbled a glass tube fitted with a screen, then a handful of evil-looking little vials painted in camouflage colors. They were vials of crack.

I stood holding the stuff in the palm of my hand, staring at it. Sloane? Could it be the same Sloane? The one from the very beginning? The idea was absurd, since my son had been only eight. Then maybe my wife too. But I couldn't force my wife's image into the picture. Instead I imagined assignations between Sloane and my adopted son, the crack and naked bodies, defiant laughter. The room they were in. Big reconnaissance boots near the bed.

At dinner that evening, while shoveling in fish sticks and coleslaw, my son offered my wife a garbled account of his favorite TV series. It was apparently about a mutant Robin Hood whose headquarters were in the New York sewers. My wife feigned interest in the account while she kept reloading his plate, every now and then injecting a mild remark designed to instruct without being critical of his sensibility. He was wearing his cream-white karate outfit with the loose half-sleeves. His hands and skin were still delicate like a girl's, but his forearms and shoulders were wiry and more mature-looking. In my mind the sight of him at the table—stuffing fish sticks into his mouth followed by hasty gulps of Slice soda, rocking his chair back and forth on two legs—alternated like a flip book with images of him with Sloane in a rented room somewhere. One of Sloane's nipples was pierced.

My wife was undressing for bed near her tulle-trimmed night table. I took one of the little vials and the pipe into our pink bathroom. To get the pieces of crack out of it, you had to pry the cap off with your teeth. Under the bathroom light, the little chunks looked slightly translucent. I tasted one of them with the tip of my tongue. It was bitter. The pipe was nothing but a glass tube, smudged with carbon, into which a piece of screen had been shoved about half an inch down from one end.

To light the crack without it rolling out of the glass tube you had to tilt your head back so that the nugget rested against the screen. As you inhaled, it sputtered and began to melt, sticking to the screen, or trickling down the sides of the tube. The white smoke streaming through the glass tube tasted cooling but poisonous, like airplane glue, and the sight of it being so instantaneously connected to the mental feel of getting high was disorienting. It went to the brain almost immediately, producing a pumped-up, cartwheeling high. A rough-and-ready excitement was everywhere. It flowed into my limbs and groin. It made me want to take things into my own hands.

I hid the pipe and the vials in the toilet paper roll, hurried back to the bedroom, and watched my wife at the mirror in her bathrobe, putting cream on her face. Her breasts drooped slightly against the pink-quilted material. Her small mouth pursed as she massaged a drop of cream into her lightly freckled skin with a circular motion. I felt as if I were seeing her for the first time.

I came up from behind, trembling, slipping my hands under the bathrobe and into her nightgown. The warmth of her skin set me moaning immediately. My hands squeezed her breasts and my fingertips wandered over her nipples. She began moaning, too, and stood, turning to kiss me. My tongue, which was slightly numb from the crack, plunged into her mouth. I pulled up her bathrobe and nightgown and

cupped her ass cheeks, parting them as one finger sought
the crevice.

Sunday breakfast. My wife in her quilted robe hums as
she cooks pancakes and bacon. My son eats his favorite
cereal, Honey Smacks, while I sip coffee and browse through
the paper. As I switch sections my boy comes up with the
kinds of remarks you'd expect from someone his age and
generation. ("I'm not into war and all that shit, like one
country over another. But, you know, I really respect the
flag. So many people died for it and shit. And they were so
young, they didn't even know what they were doing.")
Smiling, my wife and I nod to encourage his investigative
thinking. She stacks pancakes on each of our plates and
bends to kiss me. My son drowns his in syrup, before
spearing a few pieces, and then pops up, announcing that he
is leaving to play soccer. Give 'em hell! I shout, and have a
nice day! My wife stoops to wave prankishly over the edge
of the kitchen shutters as he gallops across the driveway.
I'd really like to know if his nipple is pierced too. He is
always barricading himself in the bathroom for long periods
of time. Sometimes he leaves an open jar of cold cream
behind, next to the pimple medicine.

Several times a week, after my crack ritual with one of
the vials in the bathroom, and after my wife and I have had
exhaustive sex and she has fallen into a sated sleep, I lie, sit,
or kneel near her naked body, constantly changing position
for a better view, because the drug is still circulating in my
brain. I watch her nipple rise into a strip of light and then
slant sideways as she inhales, or I stoop close to her armpits
to catch the scent. My hands search nervously over my own
body—which is getting thinner—caressing it as my throat
constricts in continual dry swallows. On my belly between
her open legs with my cock pressed against the sheet, I take
in the whole cunt, its moist folds. If she is on her stomach, I
imagine slave bracelets on her ankles, like the red discolorations on my son's legs. Then I could part her legs to fasten

each ankle to a side of the bed, start licking the backs of her knees, and slide my tongue up to the warm crevice.

The idea of my tongue buried in her as she begins to convulse is riddled into the flow of thoughts by the crack, as if by a jackhammer. I'm getting hard again. My hand moves between my legs. I'd love to have sex, but I know she is spent and wouldn't want me to wake her. She might suspect something. So I begin to jerk off, more and more furiously.

"Sloane, Sloane, Sloane . . ." I hear myself mumble repeatedly with rising titillation, keeping my eyes glued to her body. Finally, having spasmed and shot for the second time, I wipe the semen off with the sheet and fall to her side once again. I'm still racing from the crack, maybe my mind is playing tricks on me. I consider whether my son is in bed or out of the house with Sloane, whom he may meet while we are asleep. They go to the city to after-hours clubs that are open all night, where anyone of any age or any sexual persuasion can be found. And there is every kind of drug imaginable. The walls are painted black and have red light sconces. Blond wigs border black skin, silver and gold lamé frame cleavages or are used as codpieces, there are overdressed whores and bored sophisticates, half-naked transsexuals and gowned transvestites, gangsters and child prostitutes, drug dealers, punks, and gigolos. Sloane standing there is a broad back in the dark as a shaft of light catches hairs on the knuckles of one massive hand gripping the shoulder of my boy, who is in his karate outfit. The two bodies are swallowed up by the throng of bodies and pop out again over and over. Until the thought of the live body lying next to me starts me panting once more and I stroke my flaccid penis. I may not be able to come this time or even get an erection, but I keep going on and on with limbs flashing limbs, until my cock is swollen and abraded to the point of bleeding.

My son is in the den putting together a model airplane. I'm not in there. I don't watch television much anymore. My wife is napping. Silence in the house. I'm studying my nipple in the bathroom mirror. It's flat and extended, not very much to grab on to, really. What exactly would it be like to pierce it? Is an anesthetic used? I take a needle from my wife's sewing basket, grab the tip of a nipple and stretch it outward, place the point against the skin. Would I ever have the courage to run it through, Sloane? Would I be able to stand the pain, Sloane?

My wife has come tearing into the kitchen in her tennis outfit, clutching the envelope with my son's diary. Will you take a look at this, she spits. She is furious, at wit's end. Our boy isn't who we think he is, he's been pulling the wool over our eyes. She keeps pacing in circles as I pretend to read the scraps of paper for the first time. Something has to be done, she says.

She confronts him when he comes home. I keep my eyes lowered. He must know that I've known for weeks, ever since the crack disappeared.

As indulgent as my wife is with the boy, she now becomes adamant, unyielding. She chooses the medical approach. He has a drug problem that demands immediate treatment. My son disagrees with her, referring to the scraps of paper as exercises in creative writing. He accuses her of spying and barricades himself in his room.

Finally my wife slips a note with an ultimatum under his locked door. Get help, it begs, or get out. But he's barely fourteen, I point out. My wife silences me. There are places for boys his age that can handle problems like his. That night she explains "tough love" to me and cites certain magazine articles. Her ultimatum is merely meant to shock him into taking responsibility for his life. What will happen next is that he'll think it over and come around by morning. Then we can take him to see the right professionals.

But the next morning, he and some of his clothes, including the karate outfit, are gone. An hour later we are presenting the situation to a silver-haired detective, who seems to be searching my eyes, studying my slightly unsteady hands. He wrinkles his brow and slides a thumb over his square chin, assuring us that our son's leaving is a bluff, the proverbial running away from home. When he gets cold and hungry, he'll be back and ready to listen. With deliberate strokes the detective writes down the telephone number of a good drug-treatment program and hands it to me.

My wife tries to remain firm in her belief that she did not behave unreasonably. The facade begins to wilt when a week passes and there is still no sign of our boy. That night in bed, I decide to test her. I merely pronounce one word: Sloane. Her eyes compose a puzzled look, but do I see them moistening at the corners? Then she buries her face in a pillow and twists away.

I have read that the use of cocaine or crack creates a pleasure circuit in the brain. The memory of the pleasure is so intense, unfading, that you crave the substance regularly. Now that my supply is gone, I have to find other sources. I certainly don't want to get to know my suppliers, but dealing with them isn't as difficult as I thought it would be. A quick drive past a certain corner in a nearby city where our Hyundai has become recognizable: I hand the money out the window and a handful of the little vials are tossed in. One of these times I'm seized by the feeling of having glimpsed my son, a familiar sleeve protruding from the entrance to a doorway.

The little vials keep sex athletic. Yet as they accumulate, its strategies become more predictable, its plots a little repetitive. There are some strenuous lurches on either side as each of us competes to get off before the other loses interest. The fact that my naked body now looks paler and more paltry has caused concerned remarks about my health on the part of my wife on more than one occasion.

And there is still no sign of our boy. As I imagine it, he's living with Sloane. I haven't shared this conjecture with my wife, who has become too inaccessible. Where I saw need before, even if it was somewhat defended, I now see brittle resolve. She has decided to begin working full-time to take her mind off our son. Each morning after breakfast she leaves dressed in her fabric-blend skirt and blouse with a bow. She calls her job a position in human resources, or personnel, but from her description it sounds more like police work to me. It is her task to screen prospective employees, and she's become expert at spying out character defects that could keep someone from "working out."

When the deeper, less familiar voice on the phone identifies itself, we are beside ourselves with joy. He's had a change of mind. In fact, right now he's at a New Age rehabilitation center just over the state line. Can we see him? Of course we can.

The place looks like an old factory, the small-time kind that used to make Christmas ornaments or prosthetic devices. There are plenty of smiling faces and firm handshakes. We spot him coming toward us in the patient's uniform, which resembles the karate outfit, a kind of cotton pajama with a loosely belted top. And he's large now, bordering on the obese—something I find myself noticing with a smug yet embarrassed irony. His first words to both of us are, "I'm sorry," spoken in a concertedly earnest tone.

It's a progressive organization. When he was first brought in by an unidentified man, their policy was to let him stay, even though the fake name, age, and address he gave didn't check out. Now he's ready to handle contact with us again. But treatment must go on. He'll come and visit on weekends.

I'm in front of the TV watching a hockey game while my son sits at a table working on his journal. Since it is the weekend, my wife is home, baking two pies, one for dinner and one for my son to take back to the program. I can hear his pen gliding rapidly across the paper. It's kind of like having a son who is in a religious order and has come to visit. Careful and considerate. All remarks deeply thought out—well in advance.

When he leaves to wash for dinner, I spring up and leaf quickly through the journal.

"I had to surrender to a higher power. It was the only way."

"I admitted that I lost all control. And it felt super. I'm ready to live and love again now."

"Problem: is the one I love brave enough to take me on?"

After dinner he cornered me in the den, confidently repeated how happy he was that we were reunited, then sat me down across from him knee to knee. "I sense a certain uneasiness in you, Dad. Sure, I understand totally after the changes I put you and Mom through. Like I said, I'm really sorry about that. I want you to know that, like, whatever else you might happen to be dealing with right now, I've been there. It's okay that you're not willing to share yet. Nobody can help you but yourself, not even God, and not until you're ready."

And I wasn't ready to "face it" for several more months to come, until I had an episode walking up the stairs. I suddenly ran out of gas, couldn't catch my breath, and collapsed with chest pains. As I fell backward, clutching at air, I wailed out for help. No one came, and when I finally saw a face hovering above me, I croaked, "Where were you?"

"Meditating," my son answered. "I guess I didn't hear you."

The next face floating above me was the hospital doctor's, who had come to chide me for ruining a perfectly good heart.

In the meantime my wife and my son have achieved a reconciliation and a new beginning. She's been promoted at work—a good thing, seeing as I'll be in no shape to support the family for a while.

Since my son is rehabilitated, my wife wants him to move

back in the house and finish high school. She'll even consider taking him in as a boarder if he wants. He can get a part-time job and contribute some money as rent. They want to know my opinion.

Ask Sloane, I feel like saying as my eyes dart to the bathroom, thinking of the toilet paper roll where I stowed another rock of crack in case I feel like smoking tonight, just one more time.

I really can't make up my mind.

Intern's Incantation

Uh-oh: is that a cigarette, sadist? When you know I quit last week but on days like this . . . OK, let me have one, I deserve it, my head is splitting. We'll take a break, too. But you got to let me know when fifteen minutes are up 'cause I left my beeper at the goddamn nurse's station . . .

. . . What you think about 606B, dementia or lesions? Nobody can stand that raving anymore. The brain scan looked normal, so I doubt it's lesions from an opportunistic organism. And you know, once the virus starts getting past the blood-brain barrier, sensory areas can lapse for hours at a time. Then bingo, back to normal . . .

. . . Who knows what the hell's going on in his head, if he's in pain. Or maybe nature's taking care of him, he's out of it. . . . I kind of liked that guy when he got admitted, before the tube went up his nose. He's a graphic designer or something. But you know what I don't get about these gay guys? The thousand or more sexual contacts. I mean what kind of a person could have that kind of a need? . . .

. . . Whoa, wait a minute, let me see, is that a real Rolex? I got one, too. My mother-in-law sent me one for my birthday, see. So normally I don't like these pretentious name brands. But I figure what the hell, I could use a good watch, and I'm not totally adverse to the status either . . .

. . . So I'm at Robbins Ice Cream, the one down the block and across from Emergency. I mean I just had such a lust for ice cream. I was coming in on a call, a kidney stone, but I hadn't had lunch and I just wanted to stop for a quick one. How was I to know she sent me a fake from Florida?

Because when I got to the Op room, they were already wheeling him out. Weinstein was livid. So much for my mother-in-law's watches.

Hello, honey. (Her ass drives me bananas.) Listen, got any Tylenol? I haven't slept a full hour in two days. I'll stop by the station in a minute to pick up a couple. Shit, my head is killing me. Wonder if I'm getting a brain tumor. To tell you the truth, this gig is getting to me after all. Seeing them wheel 'em in and wheel 'em out one after the other.

It's a lost cause and we know it. How many years has it been, nine? And they still don't have a convincing explanation for route of infection . . . Somebody swallows the stuff, OK? you'd think barring any ulcerations, it'd make a clean entry right to the stomach and die, seeing it's supposed to be so fragile.

Hear it? There he goes again. Sounds like he's fucking cursing, or calling for his mother. Let's keep walking. I wish somebody would shut him up. Let me have a light, will you?

Anyway, it looks like it's no go on that condo. The maintenance is just not worth it. I spent all last night figuring out that the best deal right now is to stick with the share, then get out of this city. I'm thinking California, but who isn't. Who isn't thinking every goddamn thing before you are in this fucking competitive world we live in. You want to be a doctor? Right. So do two million other people!

I don't know, though. I did one thing right. I mean going into this radiology thing. It's the least messy. You look at X rays all day, occasionally you got to touch a body. Except the first six months I thought I'd go crazy. They did everything they could to knock the wind out of me. You think this stuff is arbitrary, but big brother is up there pulling the strings, looking for your weak points. I'm convinced they put me on this ward cause they thought I was some kind of fag basher. And to tell you the truth, I've never felt too easy about homos.

So every time they got a fag lying there who's so wasted he ran out of veins, they call me in. Call him, they told the nurses, he can get blood from a stone. I start talking to these guys to calm them down, and before I know it we've got a rapport going. You know me. And what I begin to realize is that most of them are people who've taken good care of their bodies, you know? athletes like me. Then one day I'm standing over this stretcher and this skeleton looks up at me and smiles. I take a good look and I realize it's this guy I used to jog with, only there's not that much of him left right now. Well the guy looks so thrilled to see me. He sticks his hand out from under the sheet and grabs my arm, won't let go. And me, I said the stupidest thing, ha ha, you know how it is in a situation like that, I said to him, I haven't seen you at the quarter mile lately. I mean what a stupid thing to say. And the guy says to me, you got to help me. So I tell him I'm doing the best I can. He says to tell the nurses to leave, and then he says shut the door and come here, so what am I supposed to do? So I go over to the bed and out comes the claw again, he grabs my arm like in a death grip, see? like this! I couldn't believe he still had that much strength. And he grits his teeth and stares me in the eye, says, you got to help me. You got to get me some medicine to get me out of this. Well, nobody can get you out of this, brother, I tell him. You can, he disagrees. He wants me to put him over the edge. Well, I got nothing against this guy, obviously, I mean I used to jog with him, but I never knew he was gay or anything, and now he wants me to jeopardize my career, you know, sneak in something to put the poor guy out of his misery. No way, brother, I got to say. But he won't let go the claw and starts pleading with me, saying please please, and when that doesn't work telling me I'm a fucking hypocrite and coming out with every curse word he can think of. And then finally, you know what he did? You won't believe this, but I'm not shitting you, I don't even like to think about it, he spits at me! Right in my face. And when that spit hit me, I went wild for a split second and I landed him one across the face. Maybe that's how the watch broke. And the claw sank away from my arm and ran out of gas. And I ran out of there. I don't even like to think about it.

I don't know. . . . A lot of careers are going to be made or lost on this one, I mean the money pouring into some of these foundations is fantastic! But with all the competition you could get lost in the crowd. My old man doesn't understand it. After all the money he sunk into this, why I don't have a sure future. Come back home, he says, and hang up a shingle. He never heard of negligence insurance, the way he talks. Did you see in that article in the *Times* by the girl M.D. from Boston, the gynecologist? She figured it all out. With insurance rates rising the same as they have in the last ten years, and rents too, we'll be out of business. And that's what we're doing thirty-four-hour shifts for, so we can give it up and get jobs as waiters? Gimme a break.

You see, the other day I was waiting in line for something, the bank, the supermarket, the drugstore, what the fuck difference does it make? Maybe it was just the heat or just a feeling that had been building up. It was a really horrible feeling, the feeling that I couldn't be waiting in line anymore. I've got to get out of here, I kept thinking, whatever it is I'm waiting for I have to have it right away, I deserve it! but somehow I feel I'm being discriminated against. The indifference of these other people in line is maddening. I mean what is there about them that they have to bottle themselves up and withdraw forever from any meaningful human contact, I kept thinking. I mean even the clothes they have put on their bodies are steeped in contempt. They have chosen these clothes to wear because they hate their own bodies and their bodies' similarities to other humans'. It was a crazy feeling. My chest felt shallow, as if my heart was beating right at the surface. I can't wait here a minute longer because my legs are turning to water. I have to sit down right here on the floor. Or I have to feel my body pressed against the cool sheets. Something is forcing me to spread my legs apart, one hand on the small of my back, my belly pressed against the sheet. I don't want to but he coaxes me in a voice that is at once soothing and authoritative. I can't exactly see his face but it is the representative of a racial type. First you must wet my cock with your mouth, and then I'm going to pierce you. It's him talking. I'm afraid it will hurt a little but his urgency is overwhelming. Some warmth from your body has infused mine with strength and longing. It is as if your blood is flowing into mine. But it is so dark in here, part of what he imagines I can see, part of what seems obvious to him is lost in shadow: the smooth golden skin, the thick corded neck, the square chin. He thinks he knows the sound of my sharp intake of breath, the pleasure that courses through my muscles without my looking up, as his belt whisks against his jeans, the heavy buckle landing with a dull clank on the floor, the dry sounds the jeans make as they slide down against the hard legs.

In some way he is about to be kind to me. But no one must see this, not even the two of us in a way. Still my eyes secretly study each half-gesture, looking for a sign of empathy, tenderness. Thank you for subtly disguising this. That we wish we would never be allowed to touch, to admire, to kiss the flat ripples of the stomach, the erect nipples and dark tuft of hair. What it would feel like to touch his face, with the gashlike scar on the cheekbone, a hard uncaring mask, eyes like bright pebbles, nostrils flared, lips pursed, a frozen mask of indifference that is usually lost in shadow.

Do not come to me at once, to where I am kneeling, huddled, crouched on the cold floor. Do not come to me, hold yourself back. He lifts his head, throws it back haughtily, imagines how this looks to me and is pleased.

Go inside us, be us, imagine how we would want it to be and become it.

So he walks forward, finally. Erect cock, scrotum jiggling slightly.

He lets us touch him. All at once, your cock is thrust between my lips, there's barely time to catch my breath. I'm forced to accept it. He supposes we must be thinking this. The odor of my leather belt is still against my hard belly. We take the head of the cock in our mouths and caress it lightly with our tongue, begin to suck it. Fall to our knees and throw heads backwards, bodies pressed against the cool partition, the moaning that travels to our ears, the hopelessness, has nothing to do with it at all. We do not exist and neither do our cocks and bodies. Only this hard cock throbbing.

We're sorry we must ask you to do this, we're sorry we have to feel this way. But we have tried so hard to be patient. We need to feel you against us, we need, if only for a few moments, to find you taking control again. We know you are not responsible for this feeling of emptiness. That you are only a human being like us. But I need to feel you taking care of me. I need to feel you demanding that I give up.

Well, fifteen minutes are up, I guess. Let's get back to our station.

Suicide Ecstasy

It was a case of extortion, a kind of love at first sight here in this electric-blue bedroom in the South Bronx, not far from "Dark Park" where the drugs are sold. The broad-shouldered youth with a part razored into his close-cropped hair stood with his lean belly pressed against the TV screen. He was slitting open a cigar with a knife blade. Between his buttocks and the wall, on a narrow bed, I sat perched and stiff, trying to avoid creaking the mattress by making the slightest move. In fact, I had strict orders not to bat an eyelash.

The boy's long, scarred hands worked swiftly. He peeled the outside leaf off the cigar and sprinkled marijuana into it. Then he pulled the cap off a bottle of crack with his teeth, tipped out the rocks, crushed them with the edge of a water glass, and added them to the marijuana. He moistened the joint with the blunt end of a pink tongue and winked at me.

Don't make a move, he warned, I wouldn't want Grandma to hear the creaking and come in to see what's up. He chuckled, then took a long drag of the joint and quickly shoved it into my mouth. Pull on it, he managed to croak out over still held breath, and I did.

Within seconds the partnership of the two drugs began to gallop through me. It was a pumped-up, exaggerated, yet meditative high. The boy was talking pell-mell, going over the evening's happenings. Most of all he couldn't get over the balls I had shown; I'd taken being the only white man on the streets of the South Bronx at three in the morning in stride, even when dudes in front of the bodega where we bought the cigars began to heckle me. Nor had I been stymied by "Dark Park" with its busted street lamps, where we went to pick up the weed; or the crack house, a semi-abandoned building guarded by an unchained pit bull and a homeboy with an iron pipe.

The boy took another draw on the joint, then tugged at his crotch through his pants, making a rhyme about his back being strong and his rod being long. Bending close to my face, he grinningly described turned-on sexual possibilities to come, provided we stayed stealthy and managed not to wake up his grandmother. His grandma was, in fact, a very light sleeper who'd require an alibi from us if she happened to decide to check out the room.

The crack in my brain was jolted into sharp relief by the marijuana as I tried to think up an alibi. Voice catching, I heard myself begin to suggest one or two. But the boy was laughing through his clenched teeth. He said she'd never believe I was a teacher or counselor from a school he used to go to, and nobody would believe I was an uncle of a girl he was going out with.

His black eyes narrowed contemptuously as he took another drag of the joint. As its red ember was reflected in them, a panic tinged with irony about my presence seemed to sweep over him; Grandma began to multiply into a host of potential intruders: a jailbird cousin, stepfathers, homeboys who hated faggots, a drug dealer. Now he was suggesting that I try to hide my leather coat under a pillow while there was still time.

Pulling my coat around me, I got ready to spring to my feet. But the boy's eyes locked with mine, forbidding me to move. Even the slightest shift might make the bed creak. Suddenly his leering panic exploded into rage. What made me think I had any excuse to be up here, anyway, he demanded, as his hand flew between my knees to find something under the mattress. Not until I heard a click did I realize it was a gun being held against my head.

At moments like this it's not a question of your whole life passing before you. What happens, rather, is a pulling back, a widening of perspective. For the first time you begin to see how seemingly unrelated events fit together. You take a second look at yourself hurtling along Forty-seventh Street and then down Madison, on the way to discuss what is known as "the product" at the office of a textbook publisher. But there is another motive for my making haste. I am trying to keep up with the person walking in front of me.

The person in question is no one I know. He is just the back of someone's head, the brim of a Kangol hat, a swell of buttocks and calves under Adidas pants. Feasibly he's a messenger or a janitor in one of the Madison Avenue buildings. But as he strides across the intersection I break into a clumsy trot, closing up the space between my overweight body and his. People might be staring at me, I dimly realize. I must have a fixed look on my face.

It is conceivable from the easy swing of his broad shoulders, corded neck, thick wrists, and cocky, alienated stride that his life has perpetually deviated from mine. I can see him as a sinewy child in the backyard of a building in the Bronx throwing a ball against a crumbling wall. Over and over he throws the ball. The mental image beneath his clenched brow is to throw it so hard that it shatters. This never happens and the wrist gets thicker and stronger.

As he strides into an office building and I hurry into mine, the image discharges. His real world fades . . . and the world takes over, contained by polished marble and revolving doors.

Fluorescent lights poach my eyes. Seated around the circular table of a conference room are casualties from a recent publishing holocaust. In the past year the company has been merged, relocated, sold, restructured, resold . . . cut back. Two of its survivors, a corporate good soldier with a Third Reich handshake, and an old, tic-laden company mouse, greet me enthusiastically. A Chanel-suited project editor smiles icily over narrowed eyes.

I have come to present a written creation, my sixth-grade science feature called "Betting on the Biosphere." We will also be looking at the accompanying three-color art.

I can hear my voice grow hollow as I read the text aloud and slides of the visuals are projected on a wall. The project editor seems fixated on one visual. It is a full-page picture of Smokey the Bear scolding a bunch of careless campers near a Winnebago. She is insisting that Smokey is too teddy-bearish and wants him redrawn as more virile and authoritarian. She also demands broad, benign smiles on all the scolded campers.

The Smokey controversy sweeps spiritedly around the table as my mind drifts back to the street, and the wrist I imagined getting thicker throwing the ball. But now the editor is demanding my opinon and the corporate soldier is urging me to come forth. If Smokey is a daddy who carries a big stick, I hear myself say, he should know how to use it. Confusion flashes into the eyes of the corporate soldier, but he wipes it away with a quick nod and clearing of the throat. Then it's settled, he says.

I am standing at a urinal on the same floor as the conference room, watching someone in one of the stalls in the mirror. All that are showing are burgundy jeans pushed down over hightops with perfectly flat, white, half-inch laces. Yet the hightops have an authority and intimacy that nothing else in my field of vision seems to have.

The hightops and burgundy jeans are strong clues as to what the rest of this person might look like. I mean only in the sense that he is probably brown-skinned or black, while his hair, if nappy rather than shiny and straight, could possibly be clipped into a precise shape that only kinky hair can hold. Perhaps he wears a favorite emblem, too, a Playboy Bunny silhouette on a hat, or on the socks, which are now concealed by the burgundy jeans.

Unable to pee, I remain at the urinal, hoping that he will stand up and come out. But he seems settled in. Though my stillness and the sound of my breathing may be making my fixation obvious, I cannot tear my eyes from the mirror or stop the images and dialogue from trickling forth. He is bounding into a cramped apartment, ignoring the *bendicion* from his wrinkled, yellow-skinned grandmother, or wolfing

down a plate of *pasteles* and a Budweiser in front of a
wrestling match on TV. Later he is playfully hoisting high a
faceless, dark-skinned adolescent girl, whose laughter rings
forth as her peg-panted legs scuff against his hard thighs and
belly.

Piss gushes forth, so I can zip up quickly and walk out,
making a forced effort for each footstep to sound casual.
Back at the conference room, the new Smokey is being
passed around the table. He's kind of a mild-looking, middle-
aged weight-lifter bear.

I'm tilting through a landscape of wind-tumbled newspaper
and exhaust fumes, my eyes wearily scanning the street for
the bank. At this time, shortly before three, it is bound to
be a pilgrimage to pettiness and anxiety, a dead wait in a
nearly unmoving line. Panty hose and running shoes,
Connecticut-student hair and knapsacks, ties and Adam's
apples are all caught in stopped time. As I stand waiting, my
desperation surges into a teary blur, until my eyes come to
rest on an anomaly. His is a hurt image. His oak-trunk neck
is covered with gold chains that hold enormous initials,
devil's tails, and a crucifix. His massive brown arms are bare
and scarred, and a stain on one of them looks like auto
grease. There is a part etched into his close-cropped hair.
Sparks of defeat seem to shoot impudently from his every
point of contact with the bank, as if a hunter-gatherer had
suddenly appeared in a leafless landscape meant only to
annihilate him.

Unlike the rest of us, this particular customer seems to
have accepted the fact that life is an endless game of waiting. He is oblivious to, or contemptuous of, this line's tortures. Biceps stained with grease, he has probably just come
from the garage where he works—no . . . most likely he
doesn't have a regular job, he got the stain working a
one-day Manpower job in the garment district unloading
trucks, and when he leaves the bank he will probably have
to give the money to the child-mother of his baby (formerly
seen hoisted in pegged pants against his belly). Then they'll

fuck and he'll tell her, "I've got to go do some more business, mamita." "See you later, Juan," she will answer.

No—not Juan, probably Raoul. And when Raoul leaves the home of the mother of his child in the Bronx he will turn left toward the poolroom instead of turning right toward the subway, as his wife thinks. His friends Tony and Carlos are already at the poolroom shooting a game; they live in a nearby hotel. Both are wearing leather bombers with fur collars because they make good money running supplies to the neighborhood crack house.

Tony and Carlos are probably itching to go make more money tonight and are trying to convince him—bare-bicepsed Raoul—to go on a crack run with them. But Raoul is hesitant and keeps nervously touching a fingertip to his razor part as they shoot pool. He is trying to stay away from the crack and having a hard time at it. He's only been back at his grandmother's about six months now, after a two-and-a-half-year stint in a church-sponsored rehabilitation center for adolescents in Kansas. Raoul chose the institution over prison, when the judge in Family Court gave in to his tearful, rosary-clutching grandmother, who pleaded that her grandson, arrested for armed robbery to support a crack habit, at least be given a chance to learn to know God.

The watery-haired teller is explaining to me that instant credit on my check is being denied due to a delay in the transfer of funds between my Super Now, Musclemarket, and Flexifund accounts. Although I am insisting that there is more than enough in the three accounts to cover the check, he is impatiently waving me in the direction of an assistant officer, who is sitting at the computer terminal covertly gabbing into a phone.

Raoul is likely to have spent the first several weeks at the center endlessly and mindlessly pumping iron. Weight lifting and the meals put muscles back on his crack-emaciated body while mandatory religious instruction went in one ear and out the other.

Then a certain Father Kilrory took an interest in him. Kilrory was a practitioner of a New Age theology he had begun to develop in the sixties. It taught the shaky believer to internalize the idea of God as something personal and individual that each carried within himself. "Each one teach one" and "To each his own" were two cornerstones of this simple humanist theology, which is bolstered by nightly discussion groups and Sunday night Quaker-style prayer meetings.

By the time of Raoul's release from the institution he would have given anything to remain longer. But this was denied, so he begged Father Kilrory to recommend continued therapy for him back in New York. To this the father responded that only one kind of therapy would now be necessary, the instant therapy of baptism. One month after his return to New York, Raoul, no longer a minor, chose to have himself instructed and baptized and found a full-time job breaking boxes in a factory.

The pearly nails of the assistant officer click with blasé familiarity over the computer keys, her other hand holding the phone as she chats with someone named Adele about a recent cruise to an island where the ocean liner was met by natives in hollow tree-trunk canoes who sold souvenirs made out of iguana hide. Peeking at the computer screen, she muffles the phone receiver ceremoniously, informing me that the system is down. In response I throw a frantic expression into my eyes. She extracts a quartz crystal from her drawer and places it in the palm of my hand. Hold this and concentrate on the energy, she explains, the system will be back up in no time. With a masterful half smile she returns to her phone conversation, describing a complex reducing salon on the luxury liner.

One month after his baptism he is arrested. He is stopped at Thirty-fourth and Sixth for jumping a turnstile on the PATH train. But unbeknownst to him, a major cleanup of the subways, focusing on homeless people of color, is in progress. Unwilling to get saddled with a fine when he has almost saved enough money for a church outing to Atlantic City, Raoul jokingly gives Ronald Reagan as his name to the cop and says his address is the White House. For this he is written up as homeless, possibly unbalanced, and resisting arrest. He is taken to the Midtown South precinct for a computer check, but the computers are down.

By morning the precinct's bullpen is filled to standing room only. Because of the overload, he is not removed from the cell for thirty-six more hours and doesn't receive any food in the interim. Unfortunately the fact that the computer was down when he was brought in means that his name has never been entered. No one has any idea what he was arrested for and, out of a better solution, he is sent over to Central Booking. At Central Booking the overload is such that charges are being retroactively thought up for those few for whom no report can be found. Raoul is charged with vagrancy and resisting arrest and taken to a cell in the courthouse. Here he dozes off for a few moments while another inmate slips off his sneakers and puts a tattered, smaller pair back on his feet.

It is not until three days later that he is brought before a judge. Weary of the constant influx from the cleanup, the judge listlessly sentences him to ten days at Rikers Island. Raoul is brought to cell block C-76 that morning, his heels hanging over the backs of his too small sneakers. To his surprise, it is hard to distinguish between inmates and guards. They seem to be on familiar terms with one another, and some of the inmates are highly favored over others.

A guard comes into the ward to do a count, and one inmate jokingly calls out random numbers to distract him. The guard flies into a rage and starts to beat the inmate savagely. Suddenly two other prisoners jump into the melee. But instead of fighting the guard, they are enthusiastically beating and kicking the other prisoner.

Cowering against the wall in his too small sneakers, Raoul clams up, puts a blank look on his face; later he mentions the incident to another prisoner, careful to use a nonchalant tone. The man explains that the guard and the prisoners who beat up the other inmate had been smoking crack together.

The next morning Raoul is in the showers when he recognizes the voices of the inmates who had fought on the side of the guard. As he walks out, one playfully encircles his neck and refers to him in Spanish feminine diminutives. Raoul suggests he go shit on the cunt of his mother, and the other prisoner's fist flies toward his face. Raoul falls. All he remembers then is a folding chair being slammed across his ass and back over and over again.

Heart pounding, I am wandering aimlessly down Madison toward Forty-second, and then west, with my hard-won money, dramatically ruing my meaningless day and boring work responsibilities. The story of my life is one of severe deprivation: my mind posing on cathexis points that bring me into contact with other human beings only for a moment; a brown wrist or biceps, a pair of hightops, the edge of a Kangol hat. It is apparent that the vitality and tragedy of others will always be closed off to me most of the time; yet it is too late to keep back this insane flood of words and images. On and on I clumsily trudge, lost in hopeless, yearning bitterness. On and on I trudge, toward Eighth Avenue.

In less than an hour after his return from Rikers, he got hold of a crack pipe. After the last ten days it seemed the most logical, the smartest thing to do. His reconciliation with the drug was like meeting the father all over again. And what had been driven out returned tyrannically, determined to take a more tenacious hold.

Within a month Raoul began to find it difficult to get to his job in the morning to break boxes at the factory. When he did show up, he sometimes had to spend the greater part of the day nursing his nerves on large quantities of milk. Church outings to Atlantic City were forgotten; he sold his blue sheepskin coat one Saturday at four in the morning, and after he was ripped off twice in "Dark Park," he got hold of a gun.

He leans down to take his shot at the pool table, wondering if Tony and Carlos's offer to run some stuff with them might not be a good idea. But since doing so would force him to admit his snowballing involvement with crack, he decides to get money tonight some other way.

He thinks of a hustler bar near Times Square where he once went with a friend. The friend had promised that it was a place to find easy money. All you had to do was let one of the faggots who went there suck your dick, and sometimes you could make him so scared of you that even that wasn't necessary. His friend hadn't been wrong. Raoul met a faggot in a toupee who took him to a hotel where you could rent by the hour. The guy gave him twenty-five dollars for a blow job that took about ten minutes. He'd been polite and come up with the money immediately, and even when Raoul sarcastically referred to him as female, he didn't seem to mind.

But this evening the bar was not very crowded. Even if it had been, the man perched in a corner would have been likely to stand out. He looked out of place here, maybe because—though far from a young man—he had a childish, bewildered look on his face. Something about him made Raoul feel he should speak to him, and as they spoke, the man stared with a strange intensity that seemed to hang on Raoul's every word. When you thought about it, the man really didn't seem to be listening to what you said but was fascinated by the way you said it, the words you used, or the way you pronounced them. It was almost as if the guy was getting off without paying, and Raoul started to resent the whole situation.

Still the man persisted, and soon Raoul became impressed by a kind of desperate respectfulness he felt coming from him. He found himself telling a little about his life in the Bronx at his grandmother's, and the man asked him whether he thought they would ever see each other again—and if they did, whether he could ever visit his neighborhood with him.

The boy seized on an improbable scheme. He would get the guy up to the neighborhood tonight, and then get money for drugs out of him once they were up there. A white guy up there alone was certainly not going to make too big a fuss.

But during the long taxi ride to the Bronx their rapport

grew. The man seemed strangely eager, even when the boy began to mention drugs. It was obvious that the guy had never been in a neighborhood like this, much less in "Dark Park" or a crack house. The evening was turning into an adventure and Raoul was becoming an enthusiastic teacher; what was more, the guy seemed quite willing to shell out money for drugs, cigars, and even a six-pack. When the man suggested they go somewhere to get high together and then have sex, the boy found himself acquiescing. There was something approving about the stranger that made it all seem okay.

He saw himself tiptoeing up the stairs of his grandmother's building with the white guy behind him. As he unlocked the door, he realized the absurdity of what he was doing. What if his grandmother woke up, or what if the guy turned out to be a narc? As soon as they were squeezed into his tiny bedroom, the image of the guy sitting on the bed in his leather coat looked wrong to him. There was something about the eyes, like they were pleading with him and hitting on him at the same time.

He tried to forget about it and rolled the crack and reefer into a joint. Then they shared it and the boy felt himself going through changes. One minute the white guy looked like an angel. Like a teacher or the father. The next minute there was something creepy, almost slimy, about him.

The boy tried to make it all right by talking, but it was as if the man were devouring every word. Soon there would be nothing left and he was going to drown. In an effort to gain control he tried to make the guy lose confidence. He said there'd be people coming in, that it was too dangerous to have sex, that he'd have to give him money, anyway. But seeing the man get frightened only began to fill him with rage.

"Who do you think you are you can come up here and spy on me," the boy blurted out. "You're the kind thinks you can take whatever you want in the world. I've seen people like you all my life and you should have a stake put through your heart. You'd cut out the heart of your own grandmother 'cause you ain't got one of your own. You're bugging out on the way us people are living and taking notes on me. It's a sin to have you in this house, and I swear on the soul of my grandmother, I'm going to shoot you dead before she finds out you were ever here."

Raoul pulled the gun out from under the mattress and held it to the man's head. Then he clicked back the trigger.

"To each his own . . ." said the man suddenly, sounding exactly like the father. And Raoul's thumb froze. The image of him faded. The bank and the conference room and my life's petty details came back into focus. And desire, which is the feeling of being alive, drooped back into namelessness.

Stations of the Cross

The priest awoke with a feeling of uneasiness. From far away, last night's occurrence winged toward him on the tones of a ringing phone. But he brushed it aside. Who could be calling? A satin-skinned boniness, whom he liked to call his spiritual son, had the new number. But the boy was passed out, at peace beside him on the sheetless mattress. Who else? Dazed as he was, he tried to remember exactly when it was that he had changed the number. It was when the calls got out of hand. When the plug was put back in the wall, rings would rattle the phone, and when the receiver was lifted, curses and threats pierced the eardrum.

The priest pulled himself from the bed and faced the arid day through a funnel of dizziness, light sifting through olive trees into the window. For a few seconds he convulsed into the customary sobs, the overwhelming plight of the human condition. His mind soared past a brief vision of agony in a garden, the snowy dome of a forehead with drops of sweat turning to blood. He saw a phone ripped out of a brown-skinned hand, then relaxed with a yawn into the familiar feel of his eternal damnation. From the open doorway to the other room came the waxy smell of dates and the stench of the old man asleep in his cane chair. His rosary would be sprawled obscenely across the floor, no doubt.

The priest stumbled to the bathroom—saw the rosary on the floor just as he'd imagined. The old man had, of course, dropped it. Curled up in a corner was the younger brother of the one now lying in the bed. Last night he had wept softly, but now he slept, with blackened feet pulled up

61

against his thin thighs. He looked in better health than his
brother, the priest remarked, and he'd be an attractive lad
someday.

Numbly he cuffed aside a spasm of shame at these thoughts,
leaned his great bulk against the sink, and nearly drank
water from it as he had when a child. Then he remembered
that the water was impure. He decided to go out. He would
get some of the old man's change to buy bottled water and
fish. Today he would borrow the old man's clerical collar
once more, also—and take one of the crucifixes for good
luck. He'd do it before the old man woke up and realized he
was trapped in his chair for the rest of the morning, with
only one or another of the brothers who might happen to
feel like helping.

Thus he moved spiritedly back toward the bedroom, his
mind divided between telescoping shame and a pulsing anticipation of roaming the streets—perhaps with this boy or
that—got up in clerical garb, for all the world to see.

But the sight of the wiry, satin-skinned body sepulchered
in shadow on the soiled mattress temporarily drove the
thought from his mind. It reminded him of last night's
tortuous dialogue. How had it all begun? He had been
explaining to this sullen, street-surviving child, who apathet-
ically sat smoking on the bed, how well he understood the
indignities and exploitations suffered by children. Why he
knew them well. He had portrayed in imagery, for his
benefit, a young friend succumbing to these deprivations in
a deplorable manner, years ago, in another land. The boy
had been someone of breathtaking charm and beauty. The
priest explained how he had tried everything in his power to
elevate the child's situation, how his obsession to help seemed
only to plunge the lad into further misfortune . . .

. . . But his companion did not seem to be listening. The
bored, heavy-lidded youth kept pulling on his cigarette, his
potential for learning still glowing so fixedly before the
priest . . . but still so unrealized . . . For instruction was the
deed that the priest desired to do most of all . . .

So he had gone on with his story, mournfully describing

how the long-ago boy, at barely seventeen, had been sent to the purgatory of prison. And during this incarceration the priest spent every waking hour on his knees praying, but to no avail. He found himself stumbling into the blackest, deepest despair. To make matters worse, he soon learned that this trod-upon flower had fallen ill. No one could say whether his fever and increasing intestinal pains were the result of the abuse of older prisoners . . . and no one was to guess that the infirmary would prove more diabolical than the cell.

Soon the other prisoners in the sick ward recovered and were released, and all that remained was the frail though still magnetic youth. His gleeful nurses and orderlies, all members of a different race than their tearful charge, expressed their delight in being able to devote all of their time to his case. But it was their serial penetration that caused the boy's peritonitis and sent him on an agonizing journey to his maker.

Thus did the priest reach the climax of his account to his young interlocutor—a climax, he explained, that was meant to be instructive. But he had not accounted for the bottomless apathy of the present object of his affections. He was stunned by the boy's absence of reaction, which may have stemmed partly from the fact that he happened to come from those peoples who play culprits in this tale of incarcerated woe. His only response to the story was to find in it an explanation for his passionate cultivation by the priest: at least you're getting back for what they did to your boy, he suggested.

Getting back? Had the priest heard right? The idea was so monstrous and such a perversion of intention, that for a moment he gazed at his sullen companion with genuine distaste. To cradle a soiled vessel in tender arms, to recover it the caresses its own mother had denied it—getting back? Certainly the boy had to understand and appreciate someday, given time and prayer . . .

An image of wood weighing an already scourged shoulder was eclipsed by darkness, as the priest noticed that the boy seemed hardly concerned with the discussion. The conversation had not touched him at all. Already he nonchalantly held a small square of paper curled in his fingers into which he tipped the mouth of a jar filled with tobacco, shavings of hashish, and free-based cocaine. Whenever the lad made up his mind to flee feeling and sense, there was nothing anyone could do. In fact, he rarely bothered to eat these days, so taken was he by his cursed, damning drugs.

Grim anticipation coiled in the priest's belly. As much as he loathed drugs that stole intelligence, skewed emotions, and could even kill, so was he well aware of sudden swoops of grace, opportunity. Perhaps the child was too thickheaded and stubborn to listen to reason—to what the priest in his confessions was trying to implant; then reason had to be forced upon him. And what better state of mind for this could there be than one in which the subject was hypnotically open to influence? Influence can only enter the mind as a drop of water will enter a moist sponge. So saturated with self-loathing at this reasoning was the priest that he made up his mind for a swift solution: he would take the drug, too.

Gazing at the human hand whose shape mirrors that of the one nailed to wood, but which was attached to his own body, the priest had seen himself reach for the smoking concoction rolled in paper, take it from the young, brown-skinned hand, and inhale it deeply. Was there any use in going over what happened next?

Perhaps not. The priest shrugged wearily, resting his eyes on the boy's sprawled form, struck by ever-brighter pebbles of light from the window. He heard the old man moan from the next room, trying to call out, but too weak. Well, today he could wait until the priest was good and ready.

Then the tones of the phone lashed out again. It was strange that the boy did not wake up and lunge to answer it as he usually did. Instead the priest stumbled to it, determined once and for all to rip the cord from the wall permanently; but he fell, and moved on his knees to pick up the receiver.

There was silence at the other end of the line, and the caller hung up with a sharp click. The priest heard this sound with a delicious irony; it was like the sting of a whip. Then he remembered last night's call, when the boy had gotten to the phone before he had. Someone—the boy or his brother—had plugged it back in.

One of the tormentors was calling—one of the boy's perverters or whores. Although the boy had been warned over and over never to give the number out, callers had become legion. There was always an excuse. Either the crude voice supposedly had work for the boy, or the female voice was a cousin with news of his mother. Until finally, a single voice returned again and again. It haunted the priest constantly. It was a nameless voice that the boy denied knowing each time. He wanted to make the priest believe that it was many people. And the voice rapidly changed from distant politeness to cooing irony to acid threats.

The caller coveted the boy. The priest even had reason to suspect that he was a pimp, that the boy worked for him when he could get out. And then there was the jewelry, the watch, that had suddenly disappeared from the house. Could it be that the boy was stealing from them and funneling it to the voice on the line? It was an idea that filled the father with helpless rage. Didn't the boy have everything he needed right here: food, shelter, understanding? He had to get him away from the phone, rip it out of his hand, pin the slender body against the wall.

Once released from the priest's arms, the child said nothing to defend himself. Passively he marched back to the bed as if he agreed with his accuser. He lit a cigarette. The priest looked on, fascinated through the merciful buffer of the drugs.

The boy got up and started pacing. Then movement through space extended into writhings, he clenched his fists and hunched his shoulders; suddenly the arms were flung apart and backwards as if nailed there, and a stony look transfixed the eyes, as the boy halted inches from the priest, staring in a convulsed manner into the face of that one who would dare seek imprint in his psyche.

The priest's arm swept out and the gaunt face became a vibrating blur. When the priest was finished, he was filled with horror at the sight of his own handiwork. The pouting mouth and aquiline nose were obliterated in a sea of blood, an eye had become gleamingly raw. The priest fled to the bathroom and wrung his hands, gazing into the mirror with disbelief and self-loathing. Then through the door he watched the boy lurch to the bed and fold like a released spring.

Now was the time to move, he realized. For at this moment and at this moment only would the will of the shattered boy be open to what was most vulnerable in the priest himself. An intensely pure tenderness welled up inside him and swept him to the bed, where the youngster lay, wings folded in a swoon.

And the rest must be left in shadow. For duty calls. The moans of the awakened octogenarian—a priest who once guided him as well as caring for a large parish—fill the air. He'll give the old man a pill before he goes out.

With brisk purposefulness, he goes to the other room to choose the black garment and white collar and to get the barbiturates. He stoops gently to pat the tousled head of the little brother upon which he imagines a peculiar crown.

But the vial of pills is nowhere to be found. And as the priest searches for them, the older brother opens a swollen eye, uncurls fingers tinted red by a handful of sleeping pills, and receives each flat, thin lozenge on an outstretched tongue.

Dust, Angel

Real Power: I'm talking about you and me. Us wearing
tuxedos and me showing up in a white one. You got to dress
up this way for this restaurant, it's the most high-class one
you can think of. You're a big coke dealer and so am I.
Though I show up smiling, it's just that I don't want to get
my white tuxedo dirty, but somebody is giving you lip, so I
have to take his fucking face and make mincemeat out of it.

Nobody talks to you that way, not to you. You understand what I mean when I tell you we were all *padrinos*. It
was a bugged-out dream, I can't remember all of it.

The first one I ever had about you.

You never think I'm ever thinking about anything, do
you. But you don't know how much I'm always thinking,
thoughts spinning around like a revolving door spitting things
out.

Making people do things to me they wouldn't do really,
dressing them up and peeling them down, putting weapons
in their hands, making them too nice or ready to murder
me, saying you lied to me yesterday.

Did you?

My mind so full of so much shit like bees buzzing round
and round the same branch.

Have you ever seen that? A whole colony of bees settling on a branch.

Lucky you didn't walk into it 'cause I wouldn't want to see you get hurt.

And there would be too many bees all at once to punch each of them out.

Can you see me spinning round and round, knocking those bees off one at a time like a wheel that goes *whirrr?* My mind churning out cartoons into the black air.

One of them's my dog Kuchi, used to yap around my mother's ankles, yapping and yapping at our old man because he's beating her up.

One of them's my little brother with his pants falling off his butt.

The other's a fish that used to be in a tank in somebody's house. If you stick your lips right up against the glass, this fish would come and stick his lips against the glass, too, right up to you.

The glass would feel cold.

Wonder where the fish is now.

Probably dead.

You keep thinking about things and you don't know why. The thoughts swim around looking for a place to get out but they can't find it, maybe you made them up.

Like this one: I'm so little I'm in a shoebox: that was my little bed. The shoebox is on the floor and Kuchi's coming over to see what's in it, then he begins to lick me and at first it feels good.

Did you ever get licked all over?

Now it's kind of weird 'cause Kuchi has taken a little bite of me.

Now he's going to eat my leg off, somebody's got to stop him.

When a dog tries to eat a baby it doesn't really hurt. The teeth sink right through the soft skin, you know, sometimes a cat will eat her baby but when they found that they took me away from my mother.

Then when I was four they gave me back.

Hand me that pillow. Now let me tell you what I was thinking about that dream.

The coolest Mafia man. The best scarface walking into a restaurant that's so shiny you need sunglasses to look at the silverware. He's on his way to meet the godfather because he's his ace and number-one boy walking right in just as they bring out the steak on the silver plate, or is it a snake? Maybe it's a snake on a silver platter coiled up like rope. You're wearing a black tuxedo and I'm wearing the white one, remember. Can I have some coke, I say.

You pull out your silver blade and open up the diamond-studded box and fix me a line, everybody in the restaurant is watching but nobody dares to say anything, nobody except one person who is thinking of saying something. It's a guy that's so jealous he just can't stand to see us set up like this and I feel—

Did you ever look in the mirror and what you saw in the

glass, suddenly for a moment you pretended it was someone else and he makes a face at you and you have to keep from smashing your fist into the mirror—

Well, I felt like that when I looked at this dude that's jealous of us. It's as if I saw him in the mirror and I really didn't like what I saw.

It's the worst feeling you can imagine.

I'm glad I remembered to bring my piece.

That's what this bulge in my tuxedo pants pocket is, by the way.

I had asked you to carry it but you said, if I had a big bulge in my pants pocket everybody would look because they're not used to seeing it, but you, kid, they're used to seeing a big bulge there anyway, so you put it in your pocket.

And you keep looking at that bulge in my pocket and feeling safe—'cause you know what's in there and it's going to keep anybody from giving us any trouble.

Hairy scary moby dick, that's what's in there.

So we take some more coke, you open the diamond box— was it diamond or gold?—and give it to me until the wheels spin in my head and a dog is yapping there. I wish he'd shut up, he's making the walls spin, we hated what was going on, which is why he used to run around her ankles yapping.

And now the guy in the mirror, he's standing in front of you, sir, and my hand's on my piece, I've got to protect you.

But what I can't understand, what I can't even look at is you're reaching out and laying your hand on him, nice: the way you do to me. So that he looks more and more like me till I can't stand it anymore, and now I'm the one who's jealous, I want to smash the mirror with my fist that fucking traitor, I'd like to cut off his ears and stuff them in his mouth because he's not worth hearing a kind word from you, he doesn't deserve it, don't let him near you, he doesn't deserve it, don't listen to him because he's rotten.

He might bite your balls off.

Don't get mad at me, it was only a dream. Press your hand against my forehead like that, it makes me feel better.

I should start working out more, shouldn't I.

Then I could take you easy, if I wanted to.

Only kidding.
I'd protect you.

Except sometimes I feel a little mad at you because you're always telling me what to do—yap-yapping at me all the time, till I get a little sick of hearing it or you want to have sex when I don't which to be perfectly honest is quite a few times even though I say okay and you say if you don't want to and I say just let me finish this beer.

Don't get mad.
I do have feelings for you.
I appreciate all you did and shit.
Pass me a beer, would you.

Yapping and yapping in my head until the nightmare was finished, 'cause there's nothing you can do while it's happening, if somebody you care about is wearing a black tuxedo in the most high-class Mafia restaurant in the world and you are his ace and the two of you are ruling the fucking world but suddenly he is reaching out to touch the fucking asshole that does not even respect him, there's no way of waking up from the nightmare.

Just leave me alone when I get like that, don't take it personally, I don't even know you're in the room, I can't get the dream out of my head and I begin to believe that it's really happening, I know it's not your fault but I'll kill you if you come near me.

I didn't mean you, I meant him.

Give me a kiss.

I'll tell you about that fish—listen to me—I'll tell you all about him: he can't see. That's why he comes up real close when you put your lips on the glass, he comes to see what it is. Then when he does there's something in his lips that makes them stick to the glass, and he's stuck there—isn't that bugged out—and you think he's kissing you. But he's stuck there and can't get away.

If I was that fish, and I had a fist, I'd smash it right through that glass, then the water would come spilling out all over that guy's kisser and wouldn't he be surprised, maybe his mouth would fall open, and I'd slide inside it— swim right through him and punch him in the guts with my fins.

Or bite his balls off.

Imagine a fish biting a guy's balls off. It's bugged out, isn't it.

I suppose I should tell you that when I was in the bar the other night I met this dude and he said I have cocaine, why don't you come over we'll do some. When I came over he did have coke and he kept trying to tell me to take off my gloves and I wouldn't. He even got my pants off but I wouldn't take off the gloves. Then finally he said why don't you take off one glove, I promise you won't have to take the other off.

I took it off.

We got it on and he gave me some money which I gave most of it to you, you remember you asked me have I got any of the cash you gave me and I gave you back three fins? Well, that wasn't what you gave me I spent that but what I gave you back I got from him.

Then tonight I saw him in the bar and I said hey I want my glove back, I left it at your house, I forgot to take it.

And he said I threw it away.

You couldn't have thrown it away I said because you made me take it off. You couldn't have thrown it away.

Well, I did he said that money I gave you was worth a lot more than that stupid glove anyway.

I grabbed him by the shirt and slammed him up against the bar, said give me my fucking glove, you stole my fucking glove you bastard.

And he said what's the big deal about a glove. Then he got scared for a second and pulled out a twenty and said here will this take care of it, and I took it and said it would but I didn't really feel that way.

And he said, can I buy you a drink my friend?

And I said I'd love one thank you.

And he said I really had a good time with you.

It'll be better the second time I said and he went and talked to somebody else.

To tell you the truth I had another dream. We were at a shopping mall and you were going to buy me a new pair of Adidas. Where are they I said, I want to try them on, give me the box, oh you said I left the box inside the store. So I went to wait for you in the parking lot and then I kept walking, there was a tree by the side and on a branch hanging from it was a whole bunch of bees. The bees had formed in the shape of a head like your face and the mouth was open like a big hole as if to kiss me and I laughed.

Sometimes I wish they'd put me in a shoebox and leave me there for a while with the cover on it—just leave me alone—I don't want to watch what some people do to other people. That little pup always knew when something wasn't right.

I guess I should tell you I went home with that guy again tonight. Please don't be mad at me. You remember you bought me those gloves.

After he gave me the bill and bought me the drink and then he came back he was a little high and he said maybe I should, maybe I should try it again. Let's go I said.

We went over to his place.

And what do you think: there was the glove lying right there on the couch where I had left it.

But I thought you threw it away.

I thought I did, he said, go ahead take it. Take your pants off.

But I wouldn't and I made him suck my dick with my pants on this time.

Afterward he said that wasn't so good, it was better last time.

I didn't say anything so he said that again. Okay, he said then no hard feelings. But I've got to get up early.

Okay, I said. I took the glove.

He said see you.

Aren't you forgetting something, aren't you forgetting to give me the money.

But I gave you twenty in the bar he said.

That was for the glove.

You got the glove back.

Look, are you going to give me some money. You said you threw the glove away.

I already gave you money. Now take the glove and get out, you lied to me anyway, it wasn't better the second time.

You lied to me, you said you threw the glove away, I said, now give me my money or I'll work your face over.

Get lost he said.

I hit him so hard he fell over and I worked his face over really good with my boot.

You're not mad at me, are you?

To tell the truth that fish was in my house. We had quite a big tank, all us kids got together and bought it and put rocks in the bottom and we bought a whole bunch of fish little by little, that tank was something, but my favorite was that fish that couldn't stop kissing.

One night the old man came home drunk and they had a fight so he picked up the tank and smashed it. The water went all everywhere and the fish were flip-flopping on the floor, but do you know that one fish's lips were still stuck to a piece of glass.

He didn't flip at all.

He was like stone stuck to glass. I guess he was scared.

I had to work that smartass over. There's no respect in this world.

He'll wake up with a face the size of a watermelon and he'll know better next time. He'll know not to cross me when I'm thinking of you.

I mean when I'm thinking about protecting you.

Sometimes you make me feel like I can't take it anymore, you never let up. There's a wheel in my head spitting out nightmares. It's taking everything I got to fight those nightmares. Bees are stinging me in every part of my body and I've got to take care of them one by one. But your voice is out there saying pay attention to me, can't you hear what I'm saying, I told you before.

Pay attention to you? I've got a whole hive of bees on me and I've got to punch out each of them with my fist. Get away from me or I'll kill you too.

I was talking to the bees, I mean I was talking to one of them.

Open up another beer, *padrino*, turn out the light, let's stop thinking about this. Now that's better.

In the dark like this your face hanging over me keeps changing. Something is crawling over it making it look different each moment that passes. I'd like to kiss it, too, touch it, but it keeps getting away from me.

A Black-boxes Alibi

Glints from the doctor's glasses are making my eyelids flutter, black boxes are starting to pile up one within the other. I wish the doctor would stop that steam heat. I can't hear her. That hissing noise gets inside my ears. It grinds up every thought into black dots. Now light is spitting out of the dots like pins, everything is going to be shut off suddenly, as if by a switch—

The doctor says I'm not going to faint, that I'm remembering things in a half-waking, half-dreaming state: "Things you normally can't or don't want to remember." That my fall into the spitting black spots is just the normal process of falling into sleep. But the second before unconsciousness is more horrible than any memory, Doctor. And far worse than any daydream or nightmare. A dreadful logic seems to take over, and incidents that have nothing to do with each other creep together into accusations . . .

"Maybe you're feeling the medication," suggests the doctor. She draws the heel of her shoe against the ankle of the other foot so that the hem is lifted slightly off the knee . . . and tilts her head to one shoulder . . . The doctor's mouth opens, closes, as she explains that I'm merely experiencing what's called a hypnogogic state, that the injection she gave me . . . But her voice can't really be made out, overlapped by the whisper of the radiator . . . which seems as if it's coming out of me.

"It's your own breathing you're listening to."

The doctor's voice tries to be reassuring before it's ground up by jackhammers. And the air around it congeals into

oval swellings . . . like white swells of skin creased by some
tight material . . . Swellings around a red, smiling mouth
that glints like the ruby eye on H's barbaric-looking arm
bracelet . . .

In fact, H *was* smiling at me.

Her frail white knees swayed together, hinting of impa-
tience . . . of too much to drink, especially with the shoe
slipped off the heel of one foot. It hung there like a black
teardrop, oval and shiny.

H is smiling, explaining the difficulties in her marriage,
owing to her husband's disability. She has gotten into the
habit of spending hours alone without telling anyone. Except for me, she tells me. She jabs at the shiny olive in her
cocktail with her fingernails, while her black pinpricked
pupils spiral into me like drills . . . or like long, glittering
pins . . .

"Sometimes I'm afraid I've used his sickness to buy my
independence," she sighs, "used it as an excuse for a career
as a fashion designer."

Her husband is sitting all the way at the other end of the
large room. She speaks under her breath. His eyes are
focused on the tiny plaque on his lap. He is holding a sharp
stylus, absorbed in his miniature engraving of his wife. He
looks up. The look hangs between us in midair . . . until the
head sinks down again . . . while H holds the pose that he
has suggested for her, and the hem of her dress begins to
creep above her knee.

Clamped between two darkened fingernails, an olive
gleams, disappears. Ice clinks. She takes a sip of her fourth
drink. A quiver runs through her husband's body. The stylus drops out of his hand . . . Had he heard . . . ? She gets
up, picks up the stylus, puts it back in his hand, sits down
again. Clutching a pencil in a thin hand half obscured by a
large ring, she continues to speak in the same amiable tone
about the gloves she's designed, the ones I'm to display, my
reason for being here.

Their living room is filled with her sketches: gloves for all occasions. And with his work: hundreds of tiny miniatures of her.

The hand with the darkened fingernails picks up the cocktail glass . . . sets it down . . . lights a cigarette . . . Slowly the face unfocuses in a screen of smoke. The glass rises into the smoke, disappears. The ice clinks . . . The uninterrupted whisper of steam heat changes the walls to a powder that seems to float in the air. On the powder, H's designs and the miniatures of her etched by her husband are quivering . . . in the smoke.

She stands up suddenly. What has her husband asked for? Her cotton hands flutter above his head. She takes the engraving from his lap and sets it on the table. Her voice gets louder as she moves toward the dressing room. What is the reason for her sudden excitement?

You ask me what she's saying, Doctor . . . ?

It would only bore you, it would only sound so very banal to you . . . since it's just a conversation about fashion:

small talk about the problem of falling asleep . . .

There is really no substitute for a good night's sleep or afternoon beauty rest, is there? And it's clear that modern life is making it harder and harder to "get away from it all," don't you agree? Perhaps the use of a sleep mask . . . after all, it's safer than prescription drugs. And it's certainly less expensive than hours spent on a psychiatrist's couch . . . please don't take offense . . . To be blindfolded during sleep is astonishingly . . . refreshing and . . .

To be perfectly honest, sleep is becoming more and more of a problem for me. As soon as the lights are turned off all at once in this wing, everyone is plunged into utter blackness. I lie on my bed listening to others' snores in the ward. The room is blacker than the inside of a camera. The floor falls away, but I'm only sinking into another sort of room, deeper, blacker . . . a black box . . . And inside it is another, and another . . . until an enormous stab of light, too bright to make out the figures it reveals, clubs me into unconsciousness. When I first wake up I don't know whether I've passed out or fallen asleep. I can't move my arms or

legs, my lips are stuck to my teeth. The overhead lights are
white coals sitting on my eyes. You're bending over my bed,
Doctor, just a pink shape, shiny pearls, a blurred oval of a
face. Your glasses, if you're wearing them, are like long
tunnels . . . black boxes piling up . . . black sparks into
which I start to fall all over again.

In fact, these fainting fits got so bad that H's husband
suggested I stop visiting them . . . I'd fainted more than
once in front of other guests—I couldn't remember anything
when I woke up . . . But I kept coming back to see them,
maybe because H said she sympathized. She too sometimes
found it hard to get her breath, to keep her balance, she
would tell me—as she mixed me a cocktail and handed it to
me and watched me drink it with the same concentration
with which she designed the long dark gloves . . . until the
glittering pin in her red hair made me squint, hurt my eyes
. . . Why didn't the police question H about the ingredients
in her cocktails, I keep wondering . . . What I didn't tell
them is that they—H and her husband—asked some of us to
pose for photos . . . just as a party game. The same ones
they used in court . . . And sometimes, when I looked at a
photo that had been taken, for which I couldn't remember
posing—I often couldn't remember what happened before I
fainted—no one wanted to say whether the pose was real or
faked. Could I really have been doing that? I asked. H let
out a loud laugh . . . and her eyes were like dull pebbles . . .

The phone's ringing. But you're not answering it, are
you? The black phone on your desk is ringing and you're
not getting up to answer it. Shiny, black, that phone continues to ring in a sleepless room. A room that I'd never been
in with all the lights turned off . . . H's husband said I'd
fainted, and because they were afraid to let me go home
alone, they put me on the sofa in the room with all the
etchings and tiny engravings. And they turned out all the
lights . . . and left me alone for what seemed like hours,
until I held two cushions against my ears, to get away from
the white hiss of the steam heat. And then suddenly the
phone rang—would you please answer that phone!—I noise-

lessly edged the receiver off the hook and I pressed it to my
cheek . . . but there was no voice . . . nothing. Only a tiny
rubbing sound—or was it breathing? yes, breathing—complicated by an occasional thud or squeak . . . like the noise of
H's husband's rubber-tipped crutch on the marble floor of
her dressing room. Yes, that's it: light thuds, squeaks, a
pause . . . more of them. And the breathing was interrupted
by one sharp, quick moan, after which it started again faster
. . . laced with the powdery whisper of the radiator. While
the thuds and squeaks grew faster, louder . . . Then quieter
. . . after which they suddenly grew louder again.

It was her husband making his way back and forth between the telephone and some other point, with that painful
walk of his . . . bringing her pieces of clothing or a hair-
brush, I imagine. She'd said it that night in a low voice: "He
just doesn't feel useful anymore. Sometimes I ask him to
help me get dressed, just to make him think that he is . . ."
That sideways swing of the hip that seems as if it's going to
dislocate the thigh from the socket at each step . . . I must
admit that the thought of H's husband's disability bewilders
me. What exactly would it look like if revealed? At times
the leg jerks sideways in its socket, so suddenly that it would
be impossible to move at all without a crutch, at other times
the outward twist of the pelvis is not enough to inhibit
forward movement seriously, the walk looks almost normal
. . . except for that horrible squeaking . . . Only the sound
of the attendant's rubber-soled shoes on the tiled floor, you
say?

Then what about the conversation? Soon it will begin all
over again. The talk about the eye bandage—or sleep
mask—or blindfold, whatever she first called it—worn to
induce sleep: which is effective, but not nearly so much as
one that deadens all sound too. It is as if a familiar story
were unfolding itself almost automatically . . . it being clear
that the fast pace of modern life is making it impossible to
"get away from it all . . ." Had she really admitted to a
certain pleasure in being blindfolded? Perhaps. It was safer
than drugs and cheaper than hours spent on the psychia-

trist's couch . . . Through the thick smoke her expression could barely be made out. The face looked like a blurred moon . . . or as if there were no face, merely a luminous space under the swollen coils of hair . . .

I'll show you what it seemed like. Give me those scissors, the points are blunt—I couldn't possibly hurt anyone with them. Let me have that ladies' magazine over there . . .

You take a model advertising a common household product, like this one . . . And you cut away the face . . . no! you cut away everything else, instead, like this . . . the product, all the words, the setting. And you lay the figure on this black table. Like this. Her smile is horribly compelling, isn't it? Now you don't know why she's smiling like that, do you? In imitating emotions—feelings that the rest of us are simulating when we don't even know that we are—she has at her fingertips enormous opportunities for control. And, if I could only harness that power . . . Look at the smile and imagine it multiplying, over the table, the floor . . . my lap—

That light again? Only the reflection from your glasses? Take them off for now, if you don't mind. See what you've done? You've made me nip off part of the model's left leg. That's the one H's husband was having trouble with. He had to get a new brace. This new brace prevented the possibility of the leg dislocating from the hip socket, but it transformed his barely noticeable limp into an exaggerated turnout, even with the use of the crutch . . .

I saw no reason to tell the police everything that happened that night . . . when the engraving stylus dropped out of his hand, when he screwed up his face as if he were in pain. Then she went into the dressing room with the muffling curtains to get his medicine and took me with her so that I could see the larger paintings he'd made of her . . . and sank into the cushioned love seat . . . explaining that I'd misunderstood, none of the paintings were in this room, I was to watch her posing for one instead . . . for which she began slowly preparing . . . covering her mouth with another layer of red lipstick, applying creams and rouges until the face looked like a rigid mask—

Please don't put those glasses back on! You don't need to look at your notes. No, I never said that, stop putting words into my mouth . . . claiming to be repeating exactly what I've told you. Your voice sounds rehearsed and insincere . . . Your face . . . well, it isn't a face at all, but a blinding glare, a faceless oval . . .

Maybe I should tell the police—and you—how she described the pleasures of being blindfolded . . . reminding herself of the enormous tests of patience in learning to find her way about the house by the use of touch alone. That was after we went into her beige, silk-curtained dressing room filled with the suffocating froufrou of garments over which her soft, insinuating voice could barely be heard, while her husband waited for his medicine and—

That's not true! That I was never invited into the dressing room to see any paintings, that I let myself in when no one was home, and waited for her in the mammoth closet . . . until she and her husband came in to get ready for bed . . . clicking on the tiny night-light. And every object was softened into buzzing shadows, pulverized into tiny particles. And the sound of congealed breathing could be heard over the whisper of silk and the chatter of plastic bracelets. And her husband's voice croaked, "Are you almost ready?" as he limped toward her . . .

Do the notes say, Doctor, that pinpricked pupils are drilling into me as I'm watching a skirt fastened about the ankles with a silk cord? That the tiered wig is being attached with a long golden pin to the real hair, which has been pulled back until the temples redden? And that a glove is slowly being pulled up an arm to drain it of color just as the bathrobe falls open and the horrible medical contraption attached to the hip and the thigh is suddenly revealed?

. . . that the phone rings, again . . . and that the receiver is placed on the dressing table so that whoever is on the other end can pick up every sound . . .

. . . of the head being covered with a white stocking fastened at the neck, yards of the material wrapped tighter . . .

. . . a black rubber stocking pulled over the bound features until the face suspended above the chair looks like . . .

a blank oval, a giant olive . . .

black, shiny . . . breath escaping like steam from a broken radiator.

And black boxes are spilling out of your glasses . . . one within the other, and gasps can be heard coming from the shiny oval, while the figure is straining upright, too upright on the chair. When someone limps forward, it is not to H, to help her, but to me instead, who is sinking rapidly into blackness.

The New York Rage

It was 1990, but it felt like the future. I'd been careful for a long time, avoiding the sharing of bodily fluids, testing myself regularly to prove to myself that I was not infected and was thus presentable to others on several essential levels. But Aunt Heidi was seriously ill. I hadn't been to see her for over a year, despite the fact that we lived in the same city.

Could it have been my debt to Aunt Heidi that plunged me into the black car with the number 17-9 decaled on its tinted vent window? Normally I would have hesitated—at least if I hadn't been waiting so long. Two licensed yellow cabs had stopped as I stood hunched in the cold drizzle. They'd flicked on off-duty lights and sped away when they heard I was going all the way to Castle Hill Avenue, the Bronx.

It was with a mindless sense of release of the type often experienced in this city that I perched gingerly on the leather seat, kept balance with one hand on the hang strap, and peered through the darkness at the sleeve of a camouflage jacket to suggest, "Twenty dollars?"

The car lurched forward and barreled onto FDR Drive. "Not that a few bucks matter one way or another," a drone bounced sulkily off the vinyl ceiling. "It's the kind of person, you know, makes the difference. I'm perfectly able to toss the wrong element bodily out of the car and into the gutter, where he belongs."

No meter, of course. No hack license. The price for the ride, like the driver's credibility, was negotiable. And his remarks were only the kind one got used to hearing in the city.

Cab driving had been a solid bread-and-butter profession some years ago, the life's work of family men whose greatest risk was lower-back syndrome and who harangued you with basketball scores. Now it was becoming less lucrative, more and more dangerous. The job was filled by increasing numbers of transients who rented licensed cabs for the day, and by unlicensed "gypsy" drivers who snatched up trade left by those cabbies who shunned burned-out neighborhoods.

We plunged ahead over the Willis Avenue Bridge through darkness and rain, as I sank back into the plush headrest, gazing into the green digital on the dashboard and trying to justify my long-term neglect of Aunt Heidi, bedridden in the Bronx.

Part of it, I assured myself, was the difficulty and expense of getting there. I could have taken the el all the way up to Morrison Avenue, then chanced the streets for a bus or a cab. But reading about the still-at-large Uzi sniper who had operated indiscriminately from the el a couple of months ago had taken away all my gumption.

Aunt Heidi languished in a still safe enclave surrounded by a veritable war zone. And if a nephew who repeatedly tested negative and had a bearable job as a word processor in a law firm felt he had something at stake, it was understandable that my visits had grown less frequent.

"We certainly don't want another Vietnam here."

The interjection had come from the cabdriver. He was in the midst of an involved holding-forth on the state of the nation, to which I had paid only marginal attention. It had begun, I was vaguely aware, with a cranky baiting of the "wimpy" Carter administration as the beginning of the end, then spanned erratically into an apotheosis of the eighties under Reagan, and finally bridged—manically, I thought—into one's options should there ever be a military takeover in this country.

I'd floated away again then, perhaps inspired by his monologue, but more probably as a defense against his discharge of negativity, into vague speculations on some fundamental changes going on in this country. For a long time it had seemed to me that everything was falling into the same modality. It no longer mattered whether you were middle-class, working-class, or part of the lumpen proletariat. Everyone had become contaminated by the same limp images.

Despite the fact that the media vampirized underclass physicality and dynamism, ripping off tropical colors, African music, exterminator spices, and the passionate fatality of boxing, that same energy remained a target for our projected fears; it was still a threat to the social order.

Even underclass people had become yearningly fixated on the bland, dreaming of over-aping the washed-out yuppie elegance of a Virginia Slims or accessorized *GQ* man.

"It's a dumb colored person's cliché of a rich white person. White piano, lots of Scotch, mink blanket on a king-size bed."

The driver was relating the plot of a movie he had resented. It was impossible to tell at which point it had suddenly synched with my thoughts. His gripe centered around the fact that the director was black, whereas the movie was a comedy about a rich white couple in a divorce suit fighting over possession of a co-op. I can't remember the rest.

Trapping my eyes in the rearview mirror as if sensing in them some doubt as to his qualifications as a film critic, he added suddenly, "I've got a Ph.D., you know, and I'm a member of Mensa."

Automatically, I complimented him. I infused my tone with the proper measure of enthusiasm, meanwhile wondering why his identity was so threatened that he needed these exaggerated labels to feel he could discuss a movie.

I strained to catch a look. This was the kind of person, I suspected, who would have gone to great lengths to disguise origins. All who claimed Mensa, which is supposed to be an elite organization for people of high IQ, were that way.

In the darkness I could see only the stiff collar of his camouflage jacket, yanked high, and the khaki back band of a paramilitary cap. No clue as to whom I was dealing with.

It didn't matter. In America everyone had the same identity: deprived—our only durable legacy being, in fact, that of the immigrant. It had always amused me to consider that in most veins ran the blood of someone who at one time or another had seen some form of hardship, learned to identify it solely as economic, and vowed never to be lacking again regardless of the cost.

We were barreling along Bruckner Boulevard. Through the rain I could see the silhouettes of the projects. "Motherfucking public housing. It's nothing but a drug supermarket now," the driver muttered. "I wouldn't take any fare there. Get a gun put to my head."

As he spoke, I imagined those apartments filling up with larger and larger phantom families as the wrecking balls of the future reshaped the city into one monotonous skyline. But he kept gesticulating impatiently through the window at the sleazy landscape, comparing it to the Bronx of years ago, when he grew up. And the hand looked orthopedic, due, in all probability, to the sleek and molded effect of a shiny black leather glove that gleamed in the darkness. Drugs, he kept repeating, waving the gloved hand, were destroying the country. Like subversive politics and mind-robbing cults, they had not, he assured me, been born on these shores.

The eyes that had fixed mine in the rearview mirror suddenly locked, this time sure of penetrating my reserve to discover the worst. The effect was all the more eerie as the eyes seemed to be surrounded by blackness. I couldn't make out the color of skin in the mirror or even the outlines of a face structure, and though I subtly strained forward, the black field remained impenetrable.

In that nervous way New Yorkers have of venting their frustrations and real opinions under the guise of agreeing with someone who has the potential to be threatening, I pushed back my thoughts with difficulty to noncommittally discuss his new topic: a raid on a cult that had been accused of drug use and infant abuse. "You'd expect some kids to be attracted to cults," I carped blandly. "They offer a certainty and a sense of belonging they can't find at home."

Many cults, I well knew without saying, were desperate attempts to forge identities that could not be co-opted. And for this reason they had elements that were destructive, purposely unjust, and illogical. As I chatted, my mind began running through a profile of a black cult I had read about. It was known as the Five Percent Nation, but the New York City police dubbed it no more than a cooperative of street gangs, responsible for some violent crimes in New York, including the murder of a Jewish storekeeper and his wife in Harlem.

Developed and propagated in prisons during the seventies as one way of promoting Islamic culture, the Five Percenters drew their name from the assertion that eighty-five percent of humanity were poor and uneducated and exploited in serfdom by a controlling ten percent. The remaining five percent were Muslims and their children—in other words, Five Percenters.

As a basic social unit, the Five Percenters had created a family system that was supposed to parallel the laws of the universe and was centered around male ascendancy and polygamy. All Muslim men were known as "suns," their one or more female life partners as "earths," and their children as "stars." Earths were denied the use of birth control because one of their primary functions was the production of offspring that would enlarge and strengthen the movement. Their male children were turned over to suns at the age of seven for Islamic instruction, but females stayed with their mother until they were old enough to be given in wedlock to a sun.

The cabdriver's banal remarks had eaten away at me. I found myself irresistibly meeting the challenge of his narrowed eyes in the mirror. The eyes had become increasingly symbolic—or should I say iconic?—for me. They had begun to represent the eyes of all the ventriloquists' dummies whose bandwagon support of the status quo prolonged everything that was wrong in this world. At the same time, a lenient voice argued that he was no different than anyone else.

A tense silence filled the cab. Then the persistent beeps of my pager rang out.

"What's that, your beeper?" the driver asked suspiciously. As we listened, the beeps tolled their galvanizing call.

With an uncontrollable thrill, I realized that it was time to stop thinking of myself as an ineffectual word processor on his way to the Bronx to see a debilitated aunt. The time had come to start thinking of myself in terms of my second, secret occupation.

I soundlessly pulled a camouflage headnet made of Spandex mesh, with eyeholes, from my jacket pocket and slipped it over my head. I clicked a button in a device that looked like a pen, released a Ninja dagger, and held its point against the neck of the driver.

"Do not lose control of the road, and do not look back," I directed in an emotionless tone, watching his black-gloved hands tighten around the steering wheel. "This vehicle is being commandeered. Take the Prospect Avenue exit."

He did as I said, silently, while I struggled to keep my excitement from avalanching into vigilantism. It was unwise, but less and less could I now repress my repulsion at his simpleminded condemnation of crime and immigrants, his petty cabdriver's political rantings. It was, of course, these shortsighted, egotistical views of law and order that had perpetuated and polarized the increasingly dangerous world we lived in. No wonder that I found it hard to suppress an image of the knife I held plunging into flesh, until all the hot air rushed out of this windbag once and for all.

But I had to stay in control, there were people counting on me. So I fired off a pell-mell series of directions that took us into the heart of the South Bronx, past the Fort Apache precinct, and onto a block that had nearly been reduced to rubble. Here, I knew, there would be little chance of drug dealers or muggers bothering to interfere with what I intended to do.

We had stopped across from a dismal park, and I could feel him trembling under the knife point. Applying a little more pressure, I said, under my breath and through clenched teeth, "Open the door."

"Wait, buddy, listen," he answered tremblingly. "What you going to do?" Stiffly he strained to glance at me but did as I said and unlatched the door. For the first time I saw his face, which was, to my surprise, that of the jowly father of grown-up children, the spitting image of the kind of old-time cabdriver I had imagined to be almost extinct.

In less than a second, my left hand had applied the tip of a stun stick to his face, and as a spark illuminated the cab for an instant, his skin seemed to stretch back to allow his eyes to bulge. Then he fell backward, his weight swinging the door open until he slipped out of the car onto the curb.

I had to act quickly. The time during which a person remains incapacitated by a stun stick varies depending upon age and the relative health of the nervous system. Before he had barely hit the curb, I had leapt out of the backseat, over his body, and behind the wheel.

What the Five Percenters had failed to realize is that avoiding affixation of enslaving identities is as easy as you dare. The best way to evade co-option is by trading in your old identity for a new start, which I had already done on several occasions.

Real as my bland and insignificant identity as a balding word processor may have been, in the sense of the hours it took and the ways in which I depended upon it for income, all of it was overlaid upon a specious core and thus essentially free of official regulation. In 1984, I had begun studying literature that taught one step by step how to change at will one's birth certificate, driver's license, passport, or Social Security number. I was perfectly capable of adding university degrees, military awards, or clerical titles to my name as well.

By being discriminating enough to answer the correct ads in magazines available to anyone on newsstands, I had gradually acquired expertise in certain skills: unarmed defensive tactics, roadblock evasion, nomadic living, resistance of interrogation techniques. I had acquainted myself with tactics of minor sabotage and demolition. Through these home

courses had also come the contacts who had involved me in
my present line of moonlighting.

In offices, hospitals, and schools, under Hathaway shirts
and Laura Ashley dresses, these contacts of mostly a certain
age were, to my astonishment, everywhere. Some had begun honing their skills as far back as the sixties with the
appearance of the infamous *Survivalist Cookbook*, a how-to
potpourri on grass-roots electronics, surveillance machines,
bugs, drugs, scramblers, and other subversive devices and
methods. Others had played a part in 1971, in the birth of
the newsletters of The Youth International Party Line, which
had disseminated diagrams of the laughingly simple "black
box" for making free long-distance calls.

Then the age of computers had begun to interlace us all in
its great matrix of information control, and old subversives
were eclipsed by a new generation of apolitical intelligence
amateurs. These computer and phone company "phreakers,"
"phrackers," and "hackers," for the pure fun of it, trashed
through phone company refuse bins to confiscate old direc-
tories containing diagrams and codes, flanked an attack
upon "autoverification"—the telephone company's greatest
secret that allows anyone to eavesdrop on any other two
parties—and uncovered all of the police, highway patrol,
federal agent, and military codes used in this country, including those for jailbreak, major disaster activation, kid-
napping, "notify news media to respond," Civil Air Patrol
intelligence, the Coast Guard, passenger air-traffic control,
power utilities, and aeronautical telephones.

This great net of illicit intelligence spread over two generations. But it was skewed in contradictory ideological directions. In fact, by the late eighties, some of the best disrupters
of information security of a few years ago were now enjoying weighty salaries working for corporations in the security
field. Nevertheless, in these times choked with infrastruc-
ture, which ideological side of the fence you were on no
longer mattered. What did matter was the fact that there
were educated people on both the left, right, and in the
middle, in our banks, government offices, schools, commod-

ities exchanges, communications fields, and welfare agencies with a legacy, however hidden, of discontent, rebellion, and subversion.

I sped through the darkness toward Manhattan, listening to the sound of my beeper going off a second time, indicating the urgency of the summons. I felt my heart open wide to take in the city. My window was cracked, and my face, from which I had removed the headnet, was bathed in the acrid air and pelted by raindrops. How much a part of this vast city I felt at that moment. I was large, as large as it was—as fatal, as erupting, and as durable. With an exultant heart I bore down harder on the gas pedal. The car bounced across potholes on FDR Drive. The motherfucker could at least have put better shocks on his car, I remember cackling.

At the east end of a block of Thirty-ninth Street in Manhattan, I crouched low in the seat, studying the front entrance to a bar at a distance of about three hundred feet. What night was it? Thursday? The usual collection of cars: cranked-up Hondas with speakers in the back window from the 150s and Broadway, a limousine or two, a jeep. A couple of whores and a crack-head leaning against one of them.

I zeroed in on the actions of the black, husky hooker in stretch pants and a sweater, her red wig wilted by the rain. From her wild gestures, I could tell she was in a heated argument with a shrunken crack-head, a white guy with a hawk's face, who stood his ground falteringly.

From the inside zippered pocket of my vest I slipped the earphones, snapping them to the sound detector, which I pulled from my jacket pocket. The device can amplify sound five thousand times, having been developed to enable hunters to hear animals at a distance of miles. Now prison guards were using it to eavesdrop on inmates. It leapt easily up the deserted block, and under the amplified sound of the rain, it brought all their words back to me.

"I'll fuck you up, sweetheart. I'm a ho, I'm a prostitute, I'm a drug dealer. You know that. I'll stab you right here, you white faggot."

"Suzie, wait, okay? I tell you I didn't house that stuff. The dude had a weapon."

"You're beamin' on that pipe out here all night, right? You been runnin' through some crazy money. Now what you telling me *he ripped me off*! Go back in that hotel and come back with my scotty. Or give me my money. I'll waste you sky-high and send you to the Klingons!"

"I'll get killed if I go back up there!"

"Shit, I'll go up there myself! I'll bust every door down till I find somebody tell me what happened to that money."

Scotty, I knew, was a word for crack. She'd sent him into the hotel to cop some and he'd come back empty-handed. Now she was threatening to go up there.

I leapt out of the car, dashed up the block and past them into the bar.

Saigon Ruby's Circle Bar is a cavernous hole tricked out in grimy red velvet and beaded curtains. Within the center of the circular bar is a fountain with plastic tropical plants lit by colored lights. Spreading outward is another circular level with pool tables, then more levels fading into the darkness.

It was, in several senses, a place of levels. From the waist up, the people milling about the room looked like any other midtown "down" crowd, with its mix of whores, dealers, johns, users, and cruisers. One could spot a tooth or a finger missing here or there, an Eighth Avenue Korean wig, a leather bomber among the olive-drab jackets worn by Vietnam vets stooped gloomily over beers at the bar.

But I knew from experience that if the eye moved subtly to another level, below the waist, to track hands—a world, or rather an oiled system of passes and exchanges, would open up. On this level everything had a purpose, was a piece of a jigsaw puzzle being fit together, as a hand dropped a vial into another palming a crumpled bill, or strayed toward a fly to trace a teasing path along the zipper. Gold chains caught the light for a second before sliding into pockets and purses; and hormone ampules, which were of use to transvestites and had been smuggled from German clinics, were dropped into silicone-filled bodices.

Buzzers behind the bar controlled access to the rest rooms, a small ballroom, and finally to rooms in the adjoining hotel. The hotel itself was a towering edifice with a public entrance on the next street, a place where hoodwinked Midwestern and European tourists, as well as happy-hour prostitutes and their tricks, rented budget rooms. But few were aware of this entrance from the bar, leading to rooms reserved for special operations.

It was here that I had made my contacts and begun my moonlighting career as a kind of domestic mercenary. For it was here that a variety of malcontents, from the left or the right, political or apolitical, operated. And in one room lay my charge, whom I had been called in to protect, and who was, as far as certain people were concerned, the final hope of all avengers, the cutter of that great reflexive knot that our society had tied. In other words, our Destroying Angel.

I shouldered my way through the sullen crowd to the bar, behind which How, Ruby Saigon's Vietnamese manager, supreme sellout and human clearinghouse, stood. In his black undertaker's suit, with his clandestine fingers always pushing or refusing to push a buzzer button, he managed to seem all-knowing and knowing nothing at the same time. He was gazing impassively into the face of an angry customer, an adolescent B-boy wearing dollar-sign jewelry.

"I said buzz me in, man! I gotta pee!" The boy wanted to smoke crack or a joint in the john.

How smiled at him with serene, blank sadism. "Oh, no. Sorry. Toilets out of order tonight."

How's eyes shifted away from the boy. He looked at me and then directed his gaze to the street.

"I know," I said under my breath. "I heard her threatening to go up there. Does she know the rooms?"

"Used to work for Yolanda," How answered with a suspenseful yet smug half smile. He was referring to the madam who had been booted from the rooms with her girls when we took over.

"Then she knows how to get to those rooms from the front entrance?"

How nodded gravely; then a mischievous twinkle flickered through his eyes.

I swept away from the bar and past the pool tables. How's timing was perfect. As my hand touched the door to the ballroom, the buzzer sounded and it clicked open. I ran through the darkened room with its broken chandeliers to another level, where a second door miraculously buzzed and clicked as soon as I touched it.

I was trotting down the dingy corridor of the special rooms in the orange light. It was nearly too late. At one end I heard the hooker screaming with rage, pounding on a door.

"Open up! I can see that light in there. I'll tear you up, you motherfucker. I want my money back!"

Wild for crack, she began to throw her body against the door over and over again. Her breasts bounced and the curls in her wig shook. Just as I reached her, the door gave way and she fell stumbling into the room.

Catching sight of the secret, she was galvanized. He faced her head-on. His enormous body was propped against the far wall, to which he had been manacled, his columnar legs spread out on the floor in a vee. Somehow he had managed to spit out the gag, even though his neck was held flush against the wall by a steel collar.

The hooker stood stock-still in her tracks. Her mouth drooped open in amazement. She gazed into the brazenly derisive and handsome face. "Shit . . ." she managed to say.

A glob of spit, inhumanly large, shot from his mouth and hit her in the face. Before she could react, I removed the blackjack from my pocket and struck her head. Her wig tumbled off and dangled from a hairpin. Then she collapsed, and the thunderous laughter of my Leviathan bellowed forth, while I knelt to bind her wrists and ankles with elastic cuffs.

The floor kept shaking with his peals of laughter. They took hold of my body and lifted me on currents of excitement. In the harsh light he seemed unbelievably large, electric, and Frankenstein-like. I looked giddily at the gag, which lay spit out on the dirty rug. Dare I try to insert it back into the howling mouth? I'd probably lose a few fingers if I did. And so, as his chains clattered with round after round of maniacal laughter, I came as reverentially close as I dared and stood there, bathing in the chilling sense of intimacy and solidarity that I felt.

I let myself be penetrated and liberated by the nihilistic aura coming from the man dubbed public enemy number one, the most incorrigible criminal in the entire correctional system. He was the avowed committer of over three thousand violent crimes, a ready attacker of his prosecutors, guards, defenders, and fellow inmates alike, a living mockery of the justice process.

Now that he had escaped from prison, sought solace with my contacts, and temporarily been contained here, he would soon be unchained, provided with every manner of weapon, and set loose on a mission to resolve the contradictions of the city. Military headquarters, hospitals, schools, and government offices would be burgled one after the other, merely to give him access.

I felt the city around me, simple and solved, for a moment unconflicted. I left him then, stopping at the bar to get someone who would put the gag back in his mouth with a metal pole and then take care of the hooker.

The thought of visiting Aunt Heidi's scrubbed and simple apartment, with its polyester café curtains and wall-to-wall carpets, seemed suddenly appealing. I went out to the street, where the rain had stopped. A hardworking Haitian with a real hack license and a gold-capped grin immediately pulled his cab over. He was desperate for a fare, no matter the destination.

A Happy Automaton

I

I was treading water in New York City when I hooked up with Custard the black albino, by way of Oklahoma, in Times Square. For two years I'd been combing hustler bars near Forty-second Street. I'd slowly dumped a career, taken up my savings, found a room in a hotel, and dropped out of a circle of well-meaning friends. Now I wandered this small maze around Eighth Avenue where no one knew my last name.

I'd seen him—Custard aka Rambo (viz tattoo on left arm)—a few times before, I suppose. Those hollow cheeks, pinholed saucer eyes, scruffy goatee were far from unusual in the places we frequented. What set Custard apart from the others, besides the fact that he was an albino, was a kind of violent yearning or dread coating every word or action. I was soon to learn that it could take control of the tender, wiry body.

But I'm getting ahead of myself. It isn't just that the chain of events is tangled in my mind, it's the fact that the beginning seems hidden and ongoing at every moment. For example, eight, maybe nine, years ago. A time of normal, banal, unrestrained pleasure seeking. Talk of a new illness that is probably sexually transmitted races through the grapevine. I am lying in bed alone, with a fever that undulates and a splitting headache. It marks the moment when I decide that I am being invaded by a deadly virus. No sense in trying to corroborate it medically or to stem its tide by a change in behavior. The sickness growing inside me has a slow will of its own.

And years before this watershed, there is a hallway in an Art Deco building. Orange light from new fifties fixtures illuminates the camel-hair cap that matches my towheaded older brother's little overcoat. He is eleven. He has come to pick me up at the optometrist, and a sudden surge of brotherly sentiment makes him put his arm over my shoulder. The gesture makes my skin crawl. Later my brother will become sadistic to animals and other children, but especially to me. I am convinced that it is all based on my repulsion of that single gesture in the hallway near the optometrist's office.

A fatal outcome of both these incidents lies far in the future—last year, in fact. His name is Sphinx. Aliases Shadow, Joey. He has a way of calling forth new tricks by arching his eyebrows quizzically. His liquid, encircled eyes remind me of a Velázquez painting. According to his story, he has no memory of his real parents. He was taken away from them while still a baby and sent upstate to a foster home. There on the farm, the Sphinx quickly became little more than one more pair of hands. On the day of his sixteenth birthday he told the old farmer who had raised him that he wanted out. He planned to go back to New York and find his half sister. The old man thought it was a dumb idea. Go, if you want to, he sighed. So Sphinx left and it was obvious they would never see each other again.

This is the probably true story he tells me the night of our first meeting under seven thousand watts of fluorescent light in Time Square's McDonald's. I am listening carefully, frozen over coffee, watching the shreds of lettuce spill over his blackened fingers. In this shadowless light his face is as blunt as a feline's, the snout almost as foreshortened.

I am walking into a dim bar perhaps a couple of days later. The person called Sphinx is sitting up front, hands in pockets, face in a deadpan. His eyebrows trigger up, and his eyes fix mine in the mirror. I buy him a drink. His fingers tremble as he takes the glass from my hand. The fingers of his other hand drum impatiently on the bar while a foot taps incessantly. He keeps talking. Whenever he pauses, his teeth begin to grind.

About a year and a half after he came to New York he got sent back upstate to a correctional facility. Maybe it was just a question of hanging out with the wrong people. There was a friend of his who had a gun. They kept talking about what it would be like to have a lot of money . . .

"Over here's the methadone clinic, Sphinx. There's this doctor works here gets paid once a month, on a Wednesday. He's a black dude, see. During lunch this doc will always cash his paycheck over there across the street, then go back on the job till four. Then he comes back out, walks to that blue Mustang over there . . ."

Sphinx is telling the doctor—a trim black man in his forties—to unlock the door of the blue car. Both he and his friend are grinning as if they have just run into a pal. Under the friend's jacket the gun remains jammed against the doctor's back.

Sphinx is lying on top of the doctor on the floor in the backseat of the car. The friend is watching outside with the gun. Sphinx finds the wallet against the man's ass, ties him up. They run.

What happens to the three or four thousand they get this way? How long will they have to enjoy it before getting caught? Sphinx's big eyes blink, not registering one word of my question. He lights a cigarette and suggests we take a walk. He leads me down a dark path of broken street lamps toward Tenth Avenue. Passing a park, he hops over a railing into bushes and unzips his fly, motioning me over.

The next night he says, Want to get high?

We go back to my hotel, I give him twenty dollars, and he leaves to get the smoke. Lying on the bed, I let my eyes float to the wavy lines of the TV. Hard to believe that giving into uncertainty can make anxiety retreat. Then only repetition is left to be dealt with.

He is taking out a glass tube. Fitting one end with a wire

screen. Then he opens one of the two tiny plastic vials. "Where's the reefer?" I ask.

"Reefer? This is crack, man. You got a lighter?"

Sphinx scowls at me when I tell him I don't, but he digs out a book of matches. Having never smoked crack, I watch him.

He does it by taking one of the "rocks" out of the little vial and putting it in the end of the glass tube, against the wire screen. As the crack is heated it melts, turning to smoke, and it actually does make a crackling sound. Then you heat the sides of the tube to turn the melted part to more smoke.

His pouting lips suck the glass stem. He takes a long pull and holds it, then lets the white smoke stream out. It smells like plastic. He takes a second pull and puts the stem down to cool. He jumps up suddenly, runs his hand through the hair on his neck, goes to the door to check the lock, sneaks back to see if the pipe is cool, hops to the window to peek out of it.

When the stem has cooled, he holds it shakily to my lips, tells me to pull slowly. He puts a match to the other end, and the white smoke begins to stream into my throat. It feels burning and numbing at the same time, like dry ice. As the smoke enters my lungs, my heart starts pounding almost instantaneously. It is a strange sensation because the tangible smoke is so immediately connected to the racing feeling of getting high.

After I take a second drag he gets up again. He strips off his tank top. Lanky arms and chest. With shaking hands, he begins to caress his crotch through the black jeans. Suddenly he lunges at me, and I collapse backward onto the bed. Our mouths fasten together as he unbuttons my shirt, kneads my chest, his hands streaming with sweat. Bulky and wide-hipped as I am, my body fits into the lithe puzzle of his—hard, bony, covered with scars and scratches. We struggle for control over one another, stopping every few moments to light the pipe, inhale the smoke, and exhale it into each others' mouths.

When I wake up he is gone. I have a rapid pulse, short shallow breathing, aching muscles, raw nipples. This will be followed, surprisingly enough, by weeks of intense well-being. Someone has pulled out a stop. Pounds begin to melt, and daily routines, like dressing myself or styling my hair, become effortless, creative, for the first time. Yet I deny that I am becoming a "crack-head." The "crack attacks," as Sphinx begins to call them, are few and far between, less than four or five a month.

. . . I'm going to rape you. Are you ready? It will be the only "man rape" in the whole history of crime. Let me get those hands behind your back and pin you to this couch here. You're not going to get away. Now I'm going to rip off your clothes and rape you.

He certainly plays along, laughing with delight as I pin his arms behind his back. And he is still laughing, but derisively, when I look up from our entwined bodies into the grim eyes of our parents. Heart pounding with embarrassment, I leap off my brother, run down the hall into my room.

Now they know.

There is the creak of the bathroom door and animated whispers from my father; laconic, bemused answers from my brother: Just don't encourage it, that's all . . . I'm not . . . We're really worried about him.

And years later I would not be exaggerating to maintain that this is one of the lenses through which weeks with Sphinx will slip by. Weeks that have a semblance of days without incident. I mean to say they have a seeming reasonableness. I may make a quip about chaos or out of nowhere admit the importance of being organized. At that moment, someone who knew me intimately would be able to see something peel off and drop away . . .

From time to time friends come to see me and Sphinx, though *friend* means something else out here. People know that I have money, but they also have to respect me because I have protection. Supposedly my boyfriend is taking care of that. *Boyfriend?* Then do we love each other? Perhaps. Sentiment, jealousy, and resentment are all extended states of mind in another, more familiar story. In that story they stretch consciousness out like pulled taffy into a narrative. Out here where I am now, the same feelings exist as spells, only for the moment and in a relation of discontinuity . . .

Sphinx is nonetheless worried about my state of mind. I'd sent him out to score get-high and he'd come back with a single vial. We opened it and found that it contained only tiny chunks of macadamia. "Shit," I heard him mumble, "ripped off by fucking Freddy."

I knew whom he meant. Freddy is a spittle-lipped Polish boy who dresses in fatigues and shaves his head. Sphinx went out to look for him but came back empty-handed.

According to Sphinx, weeks will pass before what I will tell about is supposed to have happened. We're sitting at the bar when I realize that Freddy is sitting at a table across the room eating a bowl of chili. I can feel myself leaping to my feet, pointing an accusing finger at him. "Hello, Mr. Rip-off!" I am shouting across the room for all to hear. "Sell any macadamia nuts today?"

There is silence in the bar as everyone turns to watch, Freddy's jaw freezing as he asks if I am referring to him.

"Who else?" I spit.

Freddy's body is convulsed by trembling as mine is inflated with a sense of omnipotence. As the tip of his tongue darts over his lips, he seems to lunge toward me while men on either side hold him by the arms. One is shakily trying to calm him. "Forget it, Freddy boy."

Freddy's big knuckles are growing pale on the edge of the bar stool, but I have not gone back to my seat. The Sphinx, my protector, has become ashen. As awed whispers begin to erase the silence, he leads me out. I've never seen him look so upset before.

"I can't believe how dumbass you are!"

"What do you mean? He's the one who ripped us off, isn't he? I mean I know it wasn't you holding out on me."

"Sure it was him. But that was a month ago and nobody around here remembers anything. Even I forgot about it."

"Fuck it. He's a cocksucker."

"Listen, Bruce. About a year ago I used to carry around this piece. It made me feel good. Like I used to play with the idea in my mind, if anybody looked at me funny I'd just take it out and blow 'em away."

"I don't give two fucks. I don't get ripped off!"

"Listen, Bruce. You got five dollars so I can get something to eat?"

"Sure, Sphinx, sure."

And a week later, had he really forgotten? When I mentioned the incident, the eyebrows flew into their quizzical arch, and the mouth went slack. It was the dull, wry look of a gentleman.

"Well, I'm going home," I told him. His face remained without expression.

"I mean just for a couple of days. My mother has cancer."

I flew upstate the next morning. Some of her hair had fallen out from the chemotherapy, but her eyes were aglow with the abstract idea of having a son home.

We sat in one of the more expensive local restaurants with Dad, eating canned asparagus tips under hollandaise. Mom began a conversation. "See him?"

She meant a middle-aged man who was sitting across from a pregnant woman. He looked bottom-heavy too. His thinning hair was neatly clipped in back, but his sideburns were long and fanned. For some reason he reminded me of a lawyer during the Nixon administration.

"Yes, I see him."

Mom nodded toward my black leather jacket. "See him, see you."

"What's that supposed to mean?"

"I know his mother. You're about the same age."

"Okay."

"Look how decently dressed he is. How neat his collar is." Suddenly Mom's sad eyes leapt desperately into mine, mascaraed lashes trembling. "Couldn't you try to look more like him?"

"No, I couldn't."

"Why not? I know it isn't living in New York that made you change because I've been around too. People are basically the same wherever they live. But he's sitting with his wife, isn't he? And you're sitting with your sick old parents. Wouldn't you like to be sitting where he is?"

"I don't think that would be too appropriate, Mom."

"And why not?"

"Just because."

"Because why?"

"Because I am middle-aged like him, and college-educated too. But I'm also a cocaine-using homosexual living on the fringes of crime with a nineteen-year-old ex-offender hustler. Now you tell me. Is where that guy's sitting really appropriate for me?"

Dad piped up. "Clown. Eat your asparagus."

It is probably in the very same frame of mind that I see myself standing in her garden without my shirt, looking at her enormous roses. "I was just admiring the flowers you planted," I hear myself say.

"Well, you got quite a burn, son."

"I did not, Mom."

"You sure did. Oh, my God. What's that on your arm? It's not AIDS, is it?"

"What are you talking about?"

"Good God, it's worse than AIDS. Does my son have a tattoo? Why, Bruce, why?"

"Because I like tattoos."

"You *like* them?"

"They're romantic."

"I'd hate to be the girl you go out with."

"I mean like literary romantic."

"Literary? My son the writer. He writes all over his arm, disfigures his body. Won't they love that at the Pulitzer committee."

"Did it ever occur to you that some people could find a tattoo on a man's arm sexy?"

"Sure. I know what kind of people you're talking about. I know more than you think I do. You wouldn't think, would you, that your old mother would know anything about that. But I'm going to let you in on a little secret, Son. I got something to show you on my left buttock. Excuse me for hiking up my dress and pulling down these panty hose. Go ahead. Look."

"Oh, my God, you've got a tattoo!"

"That's right. Now come close. Don't be afraid. I want you to read it."

" 'The door you open to cross my threshold of pain . . . pain?' I don't get it, Ma."

"I'm talking about ass fucking."

Bathed in sweat, I come to in the middle of the dream abruptly, to the sound of a slamming door. Sphinx has walked in with a girl of about fifteen. He says her name is Oklahoma. She has unbaked white skin, bluish-circled eyes, and stringy, dirty-blond hair.

"I was wondering, Bruce, if Oklahoma can stay here tonight since she's got no place to stay."

"All right."

Sphinx packs up the crack pipe for us. He hands it to Oklahoma, who takes a drag and begins to rap. Apparently she really has come from Oklahoma. She claims to have forgotten her real name. She remembers her arrival in New York at Port Authority in search of her boyfriend, about a month ago, where she immediately looked for a pay phone to call a shelter that asked no questions for a bed.

The number she dialed was called by many runaways. But a pimp had been able to have the calls rerouted to his own number. (A week later the ruse would be found out and reported on the evening news.) He told Oklahoma where to wait for him so he could take her to the shelter. She ended up in a hotel, where she was raped after being injected with heroin.

The pimp must have misjudged the dose because she fell into a coma. When she came to alone in the hotel, she had a vivid memory of the incident, but no recollection of her own name.

As we get high, Sphinx and Oklahoma start to kiss. He will cradle her in his arms, lavish her with caresses, lull her into believing in him. The maneuvers are far different from any he has ever tried on me during our acquaintance and lovemaking. The two get naked and climb into the bed next to me. At some point I must have fallen back asleep.

Cathy!

I awake with a start, the name ringing in my ears. Oklahoma has claimed to have discovered her real name! We are all naked in bed together. Rolling away from Sphinx, Oklahoma Cathy curls up against me. "I owe you," she sighs.

"For what?"

The Sphinx's naked body doubles up with laughter. "You don't remember, man?"

How many nights later do I come to again, feeling like the wrong thread ripped out of a fabric by the weaver, the room dark but light streaming from the open bathroom door? Squinting into it, I think I see Oklahoma Cathy's naked silhouette. Then a male body coming out of the bathroom. He glances at the bed and leaves.

"Where's the Sphinx?" I manage to call out. My mouth and throat are so coated that I can hardly speak.

"He went out. Now go back to sleep."

But when I wake up this time, I am even less than a single thread in a vast, empty grid. The sheet feels wet and grimy, caked to my thigh. A more emaciated Oklahoma Cathy in halter, short-shorts, and a different hairdo is smiling down at me. I open my cracked lips to try to speak, but a pattern of needles shooting across my face prevents me. Running my fingers over the skin around my mouth, I feel the tiny lesions.

"Don't touch," says Cathy. "They're goin' away."

"What happened?"

"You just had one toke too many. One moment you were on a roll, you helped me figure out what my real name was. Then bingo: out like a light. Do you remember yesterday? You came to then, had us laughing all night long doing imitations of your folks before you passed out again. All them sores popped up when you were sleeping, what are they, herpes, right, Custard?"

Bare-chested under his leather jacket, his face serious and pale under a tight yellow natural, Custard, aka Rambo, comes to sit at the edge of the bed. His saucer eyes keep getting lost in shadow. With a bruised-knuckled hand he touches my face lightly. "That's right, bro. Herpes. They ain't nothin' to worry about. I had a case of 'em in jail when I got knocked on the head. They'll be goin' away before you know it."

"What's he doing here? Where's Sphinx?"

"Don't talk about Sphinx," says Oklahoma Cathy. "Don't you remember how he went away soon as you got sick? And he took your bank card with him, I think."

"I want to talk to the Sphinx."

"You seen the Sphinx around?" Cathy asks Custard with a nonchalant sigh.

"Lasts I seen him was with Shorty," says Custard.

How can there be theft in a thieves' world, where possession is a parody? To whom do even our bodies belong, when self-possession exists only in the instant and when possession is only pursued for pleasure? At the bar, Shorty raises his tiny claw, which is missing part of the thumb. "Yeah, I seen Sphinx. I got something to show you." With a flourish he whips off his little baseball cap and sets it on the bar next to his Southern Comfort. Then he lowers his head to show me a four-inch bald spot with stitches.

"Tell Sphinx thanks for me, will you?"

"Sphinx? Come on," I say. "He didn't do that to you."

"No, bro, you're right. He didn't," squeaks Shorty. "But the Sphinx sent a friend. The Sphinx sent him."

"I don't believe you."

"I was coming out of the Marriott with this john, a senator always gives me ninety. They seen me walking out there with him. The friend beaned me with a lead pipe and Sphinx comes for the ninety."

"Like shit he did. I'm going to ask the Sphinx."

Shorty pulls the cap on quick again. "No, don't! It'll only cause trouble. I don't want them coming at me again."

"Okay, Shorty, don't worry. But who's this friend of Sphinx's?"

"I don't know him, pop, but I seen this dude before. He's a what-you-call-it . . . albino."

A dizzy spell dips me backward, and my face falls into a shaft of light for a moment. Shorty sees the sores.

"Yo, how come you got weird sores all over your face?" He peers up at me curiously, while my mouth remains sealed. I am only a thread in this amorphous, shifting tapestry.

I live to perpetuate the laws of the world.

II

There is no pause to put down the briefcase or take off his suit jacket. "Something's wrong," he says. "Something's wrong," says Dad again. Instinctively he goes toward the hall where the thermostat is located. Then he backtracks, goes to the kitchen and gets a flashlight. "What's wrong in this house," I hear him mumble again as he snaps on the flashlight and beams it at the thermostat. Then he bends close. Like a jeweler working through an eyepiece, he squints and trains one eye on the dial. He shifts the dial less than a millimeter. "Somebody's been fooling around with this," he says.

"Isn't it set for seventy-six?" I ask. "That's how you always have the air-conditioning. I remember it was put on seventy-six."

"It's not set for seventy-six," he says.

I am drawn to the thermostat. I peer at it over his shoulder. "It's set for seventy-six," I say.

"Ah ha," he snorts, "so you think so. But if it is left like that, it'll keep going until it gets seventy-four. The idea is to put it *here*." He shifts the dial to seventy-seven, but it really isn't seventy-seven, either. It is an infinitesimal space below the mark for seventy-seven, a position so precise that no one can find it but him.

"There," he mumbles, moving the flashlight closer. "There!" Suddenly he whips around with uncharacteristic abruptness. "I know your mother couldn't have done this because she's too sick to get out of bed. But you, you don't understand. You're wasting energy. Were you hot in here? You're crazy, it's not hot in here. Do you think it was hot in here, something is wrong with you if you think it is hot in here, go ask your mother, because it was seventy-six!"

"I—I'm not hot in here," I answer.

"Good," he sighs. "I'm glad you're here, son. Your mother is so sick and she's glad to see you. Stay for a week, why don't you."

"I won't be able to, Dad."

"I understand."

Though Custard's hands and feet are peeling from eczema, the rest of his body looks smooth and yellow, like custard. He is sitting on the edge of the bed in his underwear. He's got my shaving mirror and is trimming the edges of his sparse blond goatee. He is trying to convince me to buy some crack so that he and I can get high. His girlfriend, Oklahoma Cathy, went out about three hours ago to try to turn a trick, and there is still no sign of her.

I am unwilling to buy crack, as Custard well knows. I was out for five days the last time I smoked. I must have gone into convulsions or something. And then the herpes. Herpes is a bad sign, I explain, it has to do with the immune system. Besides, money is running low.

Custard puts the mirror down so he can rest a hand on my leg. He explains masterfully, with a smile, why I am mistaken. Did he tell me about getting the herpes all over his ass in jail after a fight? And now he's A-okay. It depends on how pure what you smoke is. None of that stuff made with ammonia. That's poison. I know where to get some pure shit. Just lay twenty or thirty on me, I'll be back.

When he gets back, he takes out the new glass stem and jams the screen tightly into it. Gallantly puts the first rock in for me. Begins to tell me about him and Oklahoma Cathy, before taking his pull. She's been his woman since she was thirteen. Then he had to leave her in Oklahoma to go West with his brother.

In his underwear again, the smoke streaming out of him, Custard struts back and forth across the carpet as the words spill out. Life is a fuckup. I fucked up my hands in Death Valley, working in a borax mine. It gets into your skin and burns cracks into it. Saw people crushed by falling slabs of borax. Me and this little Mexican cunt living in a trailer near the mine. You know those pincers on poles they use to get the cans down in grocery stores? We tightened one up. Caught rattlesnakes with it and cut off their heads and tails, chicken-fried 'em.

Reggae on the radio. Custard is talking politics. Those Jews, man, who think they can let a land go then come back to claim it, kick everybody out. And that fucking Reagan, who thinks all people have to be like him, somebody should teach that asshole a lesson and blow him away. What about poor people who don't got ranches in Santa Barbara?

Station changed. Custard is dancing. Doing an R-and-B stroll. Singing along with the words as he mimes with his hands. We used to do this in jail.

Stops. Eyes go far away. Mouth tightens into a grimace. That's right, man, I was in Sing Sing. The saucer eyes get even bigger and the pinholes look tinier. Fucking two and a half years because I had a happy trigger finger. I'm fucking not going back to that fucking place, man. I made up my mind about that. I want to get a job, go back to school.

Anger begins to flood Custard's pink, blank-eyed face. Is it jail or a job? Cathy? The mines? Does it matter?

"Tell me what's happening to you."

"I don't know, Poppa. I feel funny. I feel like I could take somebody's head and smash it, you know what I mean?"

"Of—course—I—know—what—you—mean." It's hard to speak with the crack building up in my head, inflating spaces between each word. I pull the eczemaed hands into mine, massage them. Feel the once broken, ill set bones.

"There."

"That's right, Poppa," says Custard. "It feels good, don't stop."

"I'll take care of it for you."

"Harder, I can't feel it."

"I'm massaging your hands as hard as I can, Custard."

"It feels good."

Violence shuddering through his muscle-addled spine, he has sprawled facedown on the bed, legs kicking. "Fucking goddamn, it's not fair. Massage my legs harder, bro."

"I can't take it all away from you, Custard."

"You can, Poppa, you can."

He kicks off the shorts, struggling for breath, cursing threateningly. My hands are aching from the effort of massaging his buttocks. "I can't feel it," he says.

"Yes, you can, baby." He has turned on his back now, is holding up a hard-on and trying to push my face down on it. But I am refusing to suck it without a rubber. So my hands, trembling from crack and limp from fatigue, manage to rip open the package and fit one on him. The wave breaks soon in one gigantic convulsion that takes us with it, legs closing around my neck in a scissors lock, ferocious pumping . . .

He leaps to his knees on the bed. Rips the rubber off and holds it up to the light from the television. His face is streaming sweat. His hollow eyes triumphant, exultant.

"Look! Look! How many sperm! A million? A billion? Enough to start a whole nation!" He ties a knot in the end of the rubber and throws it in my face. "Put it in the sperm bank!"

A few days later, as his head is resting on my thigh, the telephone rings for the first time. Custard wanted a telephone. Of course, it's not Oklahoma Cathy calling. She's been gone more than a week since that day she went out to

find a trick. She would have no idea that there is now a
phone in the room. I pick up the receiver.

"Hello?"

"Hello, little brother."

"How did you get my number?"

"There are ways, when you work for the government in
Washington."

"But I'm not listed."

"I told you, there are ways, that's all."

"So why are you calling?"

"I want to know how my little brother is."

"Fine."

"Are you? I doubt that. I doubt that you're fine."

"Do you now."

"Yes. And I thought I would just try to call you now
because even though it's two P.M. on a Thursday, well—I
didn't expect you to be at work, no, I didn't expect you to be
working."

"What business is it of yours?"

"Well, as it turns out, brother, it is very much my business. What you are doing with your valuable time is very
much my business, some people might say."

"Those people are wrong."

"Are they? Well, I don't know if they are. Because I
think it would be very much my business how you spend
your time when you will be living off the money our parents
slaved for. And I am out here trying to support a family."

"Your fucking family doesn't concern me, big brother.
Nor am I interested in what you think of the way I spend my
time. And as for that money our parents slaved for, I am
not living off that precious money but on my own savings,
for your information."

"Well, it's a whole new ball game now, kiddo."

"What do you mean?"

"I mean that Mom is dead and for some perverse reason
she has left you a rather substantial trust which both Dad
and I intend to oppose to the bitter end."

"Mom is dead?"

"That's right, kiddo. Be talking to you."

"Rub my ass harder, man . . . Give me that stem."

"How's that?"

"It's all right. Keep rubbing it . . . Yo, Bruce, when you first saw me, did you think I was white?"

"I don't really think about what color people are, Custard." The pale-eyed, pink skull-face looks at me with annoyed contempt. "You mean you didn't think about was I white or black?"

"I just didn't think. Could I have some of that pipe?"

"Wait a minute."

"Jesus, Custard, you're hogging it all for yourself. Give me some of that."

"Open your mouth one more time and I'll let you have this."

"Give me that pipe."

"Don't get me mad, man."

"What would happen if I did?"

"You ever been worked over before getting cornholed, Bruce? Kind of opens you up first. Happens all the time in jail. Keep rubbing my back, rub my shoulders for me."

"I don't like violence, Custard."

"Nobody does, Poppa, but sometimes it's necessary."

"When would that be?"

"Keep acting wiseass and you'll find out."

"Maybe I just will, maybe I'd like to find out."

"You know I wouldn't hurt you, Daddy, long as you keep looking out for me."

"Hmm, hmm."

"Feels good, don't stop."

"Who do you think I am, your wife or something?"

"That's right, baby. Why don't you put on Cathy's panties and walk around for me, like a real wife."

"Very funny."

"And don't talk back to me, neither. I hate a white female talks back to me."

"Whatever you say, darling."

"Keep rubbing my legs like that. Give me that pipe. C'mon, put on Cathy's panties for me, would you?"

"I'd feel silly."

"No you wouldn't. Now put on some lipstick."

III

Way back when . . . We're back at the beginning again, when the stakes were not so high. Life was a banquet then. People who were around in those days would know what I mean. Our libidos found a free, expansive structure. You know the rest. I'm talking ten, twenty years ago, before pleasure got detoured into dread. You had sex or got high when you wanted to and tried not to give it much conscious value. You wanted to be directed but thought about it as something that was just happening to you . . . So let's get high again, baby. This time it's me saying it. Custard's been out like a light since he got back at five. Why won't he wake up? The moving job must be taking a lot out of him. Too bad we need the money. Cathy has disappeared. I'm stone broke and any money from the will is years away. So c'mon, baby, wake up. I want to get high.

I walk over to the pile of clothes on the floor and pick up the industrial stapler lying next to it. The thing weighs more than an anvil and spits one-and-a-half-inch staples. Custard says he uses it to put together wooden packing boxes.

Get up, baby. You don't even look like you're breathing. Playfully I aim the gun at his ass and start to pull back the trigger. He flips around and jerks to a sitting position. "Chill, bro, I need my rest, man."

"And we're going to rest, baby. We'll get high while we rest."

"Why don't you go out and get it?"

"You know I'm no good at that, Custard. You always get the good stuff."

With a grudging sigh he puts on his jeans, his work shoes, and his leather jacket, takes twenty out from under the rug, slams the door.

I lie back with a sigh. It is almost a sigh of luxury. For the first time I am . . . But how to explain the luxury of a life virtually without choices? It is an automatic life and I am a happy automaton.

Then why must the following happen?

Custard comes back and tosses two crack vials on the bed. I pop one open and dump it into the stem. I light, I pull, there is no crackling sound. Tipping a rock from the stem into my hand, I taste it. Macadamia nut.

"Who sold you this?"

"The Sphinx," says Custard. His tone is hollow, almost dead. No clue as to whether or not he is telling the truth.

The Sphinx?

It is not the Sphinx, or Custard, or even myself pulling me off the bed, putting my clothes on. I slip the stapler under my coat. It is not my mother, my father, or my brother who brought this pain, this suffering, this betrayal down on me.

Sphinx is easy enough to spot, weaving in front of the crack house on Ninth Avenue, wobbly-kneed high, his hand jerking from the back of his neck to his pants, then back again. Those familiar old eyes. As I come toward him the eyebrows arch quizzically, just as they did that long-ago day in the mirror. But this time my hand has a plan: to fly out and cover his face and slam it against the wall of the building. Starting at the Adam's apple, the other hand begins punching its neat row of staples all the way down to the navel.

She

(with thanks to
H. Rider Haggard)

My name is Ayesha or she-who-waits, and I used to be very powerful. These tits you see are real, models for the very first drinking cup used by man. I was around before all of them, honey. Isis, Kali, Helen of Troy, Miss Thing. When things took a turn for the worse, I did what I had to do. I took the stroll on the Deuce and worked a peep show. But when I tried to boost a stereo from a regular john, he blew the whistle on me. They took me to Central Booking where I lay chained on the floor in my underwear, next to Angel, a pimp arrested for promoting prostitution of a minor.

As soon as Angel saw my tits, he swore to find me again at Rikers. The uncovering of my breasts is a sacred act pertaining to my cult, and he who would gaze upon them is mine forever. But fate is fickle. Angel went to the regular wing while people like me with tits went into protective custody.

Twice two years did I wait. And twice two thousand more would I wait again for him. I who lived among the dead. And I made all the dead my subjects with a metal mop wringer used to bust skulls.

And in my cell, which I called my tomb, or my boudoir, or my urn, or my clam, others came to see me on their bellies because they had heard that a beautiful creature who was seldom seen but who was reported to have power over all things living or dead could stand between them and a cigarette, a sandwich, or another hour alive. For I call myself she-who-waits, but they had to call me she-who-must-be-obeyed.

And in the second of the twice two years, I couldn't take it anymore. I mean, Mary, could you? And I went to the warden, who sat in a room filled with pictures of love scenes and executions and tortures, and unveiled my face, and folded my arms over my tits, and said, In this temple and slaughterhouse, which are one, will you not grant me the right to be with my beloved? I can't transfer you because you would be a threat to the other prisoners, answered the warden. You would incite them to sexual misconduct. And I answered, Why would I steal milk when I have a cow? And the warden told me that because I was not natural I would have to remain in protective custody. So I went back to my boudoir and when I was at lunch took a blunt knife and cut the bleach out of my hair. And I went back to the warden and said, Will you deny me the right to see my beloved? And he said, You are still unnatural. So I went back to my cell and wiped the shoe polish that I used for mascara and eye shadow off and when I was at the infirmary borrowed the scissors and cut off my fingernails. But the warden said, You are still unnatural. So I ripped open my shirt and held out my tits and said to the warden, Will you have me cut off these too? And when he saw this, the warden said, Transfer granted.

So the next day I was brought to my beloved's wing where I saw things most terrible. I saw a man's eye poked out for asking for a cigarette. I saw another man's cell set on fire because he made others wait for the phone. And I saw two men who fought over a third as the third hacked at his wrist with a piece of glass for fear of being left defenseless by his protector.

I saw a lion fight a crocodile and win, and the lion was my Angel, to whom I said, You are my chosen. I have waited for you from the beginning. And I washed his socks and cleaned his cell. I became his female, whereas the others had to come to us for everything and no one could touch me because I was protected. And to prove it, I took a knife and carved into the shower wall, AYESHA AND ANGEL RULE C-76 WITH TITS OF STEEL AND FISTS OF IRON. And even the corrections officers believed because they feared a riot.

Yet even when you are divine you are still the subject of a stronger power. You could just as well try to make these walls melt away as to sway this passion from its natural course. Then blame me not for wanting Samson the new inmate, whose fists were harder than Angel's and whose gaze was more ferocious. I am she who took a knife and went into the cell of Samson while he was sleeping and veiled his eyes and cut him and left before his eyes could be unveiled so that he could not see who had done it. And when he came rushing out with eyes that saw blood, I am she who whispered: Angel did it.

And Angel, being too weak to fight Samson, went into his cell to take the sheet from his bed and tear it to strips and hang himself. And I was sorry for what had happened. I wrung my hands and pulled my hair and clawed my face but could not raise him from the dead. And after Angel there was Samson. And after Samson there was Apollo and then Mohammed and Lance and Jesus and Attila, and after him another, and then another and another.

But I am she-who-waits. I am still endless and always there. While all the others must live a spell, and then they die not knowing there is no such thing as death. Not understanding that there is only change.

Recommendations for The Mass Production of Teenagers

It is completely feasible to specifically design an animal for hamburger.
—*Bob Rust in* Successful Farming, *October 1977*

PART
I

It would end with a curious charge: alienation of affection. And it happened early one morning, after three A.M., as he trudged up the street, not wearing his clerical collar. To the pimps, prostitutes, and dealers collected in front of the bus terminal and all along the avenue, he could have been any balding potential customer. This certainly wasn't the first time they'd seen a middle-aged man in a black raincoat and scuffed shoes—who looked like a salesman on the road from another town—plodding through the flotsam and jetsam of the city's red-light district. So nobody was surprised when the morose-looking man stopped to talk to a glassy-eyed, hollow-cheeked teenager, whose matchstick, tattooed arms poked from the rolled sleeves of his grimy sweatshirt.

The speeded-up kid had the lean, ravenous look of a wolf. He sucked in his cheeks, tossed the man a look, and began to walk beside him. For the boy this was a familiar scenario. He could almost guess what the mark would say next. What he didn't suspect was that the seemingly casual words coming from the hangdog face of the man were careful . . . strategic . . . And that he'd rehearsed this conversation a hundred times. Slowly the man's easy, receptive manner began to forge a link, while the boy remained unaware of the merciful trap that had been laid for him . . .

The strategy put beads of perspiration on the lined forehead of the man, who was known as Father Bob. His lips grew moist. He saw the kid's kiddishness and wolfish depravity with a kind of hopeless wonder. He felt the familiar surge of being in close touch, shoulder to shoulder, with evil . . .

Detective Perdido's regulations clicked across the tiles to the edge of the pool, toward a body covered with a beach towel patterned with yellow smile faces. In the center of the pattern, over the abdomen of the body, was the slogan HAVE A NICE DAY. The detective pressed his lips into a thin line. In one fast move he folded the towel down to reveal a face, a scar-edged patchwork of skins of various hues and various features, awkwardly welded together. "What a lousy sew job." The detective grimaced in disgust.

The body, on the other hand—now visible to the waist— was smooth and athletic, a perfect specimen of teenage manhood. Earlier that day, a family had identified it as belonging to a certain William George Champion, of South Pasadena. The body of Champion—who, coincidentally with his name, was the winner of the regional high-school decathlon—had been missing since the day his severed head had been found on Bailey Road, or Lover's Lane.

Perdido unfurled the towel still further. This was definitely the splendid body of Champion. He remembered it from the photographs.

For several months there had been a series of murders in the Pasadena area, linked only by the similarity that each corpse had been found with some part of the body missing: a nose, two ears, a mouth, chin, or eyeballs neatly severed and removed. Unfortunately the face by the side of the pool had been put together too haphazardly to determine whether it contained any of the missing features. Detective Perdido covered up the body gingerly.

"That him?" called out Miguel, his rookie assistant. Watery-eyed and nervous, the wraithlike kid sat at the edge of the pool in bathing trunks, hoping to catch a quick dip after they went through the formalities with the body. He still had his Weejuns on, and to avoid looking at the corpse, he kept his head lowered and picked the lint off his black socks.

"Looks like it to me," said Perdido.

Both Perdido and the rookie were glad it was. The strange apparition now lying lifeless by the pool had been terrorizing school yards and drive-ins for weeks with sudden and violent appearances. Because its superhuman strength seemed equaled only by its animal rage, astonished bystanders had done nothing to stop it. Understandably there had been a sigh of relief throughout Pasadena when the discovery of the corpse was reported. But the fact that no one had come forward to claim credit for destroying the beast left Detective Perdido feeling uneasy.

It was possible, the detective thought, that the killer of the beast and whoever had created him were the same person. Choosing his words carefully, he began to sketch the probable psychological makeup of this Frankenstein for the benefit of his rookie. Perdido's words pulled Miguel's attention away from his socks and sent goose bumps traveling up his bare legs.

The detective reasoned that the deranged creator of this living collage probably was to all appearances your run-of-the-mill middle-ager. A man in a black raincoat. Although trauma kept him from reconstructing his own childhood except in the most fragmented and spasmodic of fashions, undoubtedly he was obsessed by a fervent desire to relive it as he thought it should have been. This impossible dream had led him to the grotesque mistake now spread out at their feet.

To elaborate his theory, Detective Perdido began to cite a certain Statute 444, which set limits on the weight of a minor's testimony. The value of a minor's statements could never be taken as incriminating in the legal sense. Such testimony was almost considered a kind of hearsay, about which the original speaker could never be contacted. Thus, in the most legitimate of contexts, the true thoughts of minors were, for all practical purposes, unavailable. There were even certain recorded cases in which parents who had the vanity to take a child's remarks at face value were judged guilty of neglect or abuse.

"Haven't you ever noticed how everybody over the hill thinks he wasted his youth?" the detective reminded his rookie. " 'If only I had it to do over again,' they all moan.

Too late, of course. Some of 'em have babies. Run the kid through the obstacle course called life and get off by watching. It's perfectly legal. Too bad, though, that like I said, children's thoughts are unobtainable to anyone that's reached majority. So this jerk, this butcher who did this, tries to make his own kid, but one he can get a handle on. And because he wants him to be just like other kids instead of like his deranged self—what parent wouldn't—he took the parts from all these average teenagers . . . Have a good look!" He stripped the towel all the way off the corpse.

Miguel used the sweat on his palms to smooth the sides of his hair. Then he swallowed hard and forced himself to look up at the corpse. A stream of vomit began pouring out of his mouth into the turquoise water and all over his bathing trunks.

TEENAGER. Any fully developed nonadult, a concept that barely predates the Renaissance, during which licensed domination of these subjects was first asserted. The implantation of rational thoughts into them then became a laudable occupation, and specific instructions for this process were treated extensively by late medieval and early Renaissance prescriptive writers.

Aquinas was perhaps the first to assert this belief in the context of Christian terminology by affirming that irrationality in these subjects was a sign that God had made them specifically for civilized society as a whole—meaning Christianized humans—to instruct or implant. Although they never replaced the pre-Christian symbolical sacrificial vessel of the kid or lamb, imagery involving their being pierced by lances or consumed by fire slowly found its way into liturgical representations.

Despite, or perhaps as a result of, the upheavals of the Industrial Revolution, the tendency to regard them as incapable of self-determination was strengthened, culminating in several minor philosophers of the Cartesian school being the first to conceive of them as mechanistic. Put simply, they maintained that a lack of sophisticated language and thinking skills thereby made them "machines."

Freud and Darwin were the first to point out, however, that rationality is by far not the strongest measure by which to judge the functioning of any entity. Nevertheless, these discoveries did little to further the acceptance of irrationality in humans as a whole but served only to increase the teenage burden of liability for it.

Ownership of. Western law has always regarded the fully developed nonadult as highly invested property, thus affording a high degree of protection. Both local and national laws specify that they be provided with certain standard comforts, such as food and ventilation, yet conditions that may occur during the actual experiments that can be performed on them are not necessarily foreseen by regulations. Although there are established procedures for many of these experiments, subjects are officially, if not in reality, denied pain-releasing drugs during their administration.

It will become increasingly interesting to track developmental changes in these procedures as the demand for teenagers with predictably designed parameters becomes more urgent in a world of shrinking resources and exploding, promiscuous infrastructures.

At the motel room, Detective Perdido helped Miguel out of his soiled bathing trunks. "I don't feel like going swimming anymore," said the rookie, collapsing onto the bed.

"I understand, kid."

Since they were on duty, the detective kept up a business-like tone with his protégé. He cleared his throat and stationed himself at the tiny desk in the room, pushed the Bible—still a fixture in hotels and motels—aside, and began going through some photos of corpses from the morgue with deliberate concentration.

The naked rookie struggled to a standing position and lumbered dizzily to the shower. As water pelted his thin body, nausea at seeing the corpse began to fade. He began to enjoy the feeling of heat penetrating his muscles. But as his eyes followed the rivulets trickling down his skin, a familiar anxiety resurfaced. Whenever he was undressed and looked down, he hated being reminded that his thing was darker than the rest of his body.

Miguel had little comparative data from which to judge the contrast. Found near a dump on the outskirts of Bogotá as a baby and brought to Pasadena where he had spent his childhood sometimes with foster parents and sometimes in group homes, he had lived most of his formative years with Caucasians. The cocoa-colored thing in his hand seemed alien to the rest of his body, which had a more golden hue. He didn't know which of his theories about this discrepancy in body parts bothered him the most. Either he was the product of a dramatically mixed marriage, some kind of a genetic defect that showed itself as he matured (he hadn't noticed much of a color contrast until a few years ago), or else certain manipulations of the organ had poisoned it. The color was indicative of a kind of cirrhosis of the penis.

Now, as the thing, which seemed to have a will of its own, grew turgid, he wrestled with the idea of consulting a doctor. He began to finger a pimple, plumped up by the hot water, on his shoulder, to take his mind off the quandary. When it popped, his mind was able to move on to other things.

Miguel had let his mentor, the incomparable Detective Perdido, pull strings so that he could skip three months of training and become the detective's assistant. It was a lucky break, but the rookie hadn't bargained for the long hours, routine investigations, and panicky moments of climactic discovery. Today had been the acid test. His neck had been frying in the hot sun all morning as they went to filling stations, drive-ins, and malls, covering the area where the creature had last been seen. Then the call about the stiff had come in. They'd had to table lunch and rush over with the siren on.

As they neared the motel the rookie's heart had lain like a lump in his throat. Here it came: his first stiff. There was supposed to be something so creepy about this one. Kids not much younger than he being used as patches to make the thing. And a rumor that whoever was doing it pumped his victims up with chemicals first. They'd start acting weird, run away from home, never come back, or get discovered with parts of their bodies missing.

Miguel climbed out of the shower to check out his reflection in the mirror while he dried himself. This time he was careful to keep his eyes off the thing. Using his nails to arrange the few hairs in the middle of his chest into a vee, he sucked in his stomach and flexed the pec nearer the mirror.

Yuk. Nothing turned out how you thought it would. For the past six years all he had dreamed about was being a detective like Mr. Perdido. They'd met when Detective Perdido was first assigned to the runaway unit of the Pasadena Police Department. Miguel had been caught trying to jump the Rhythm Rush train at the amusement park, after running away from his group home. As soon as the detective discovered him in juvenile detention, the fate of the two was sealed. Something about the eyes, was the way Perdido explained it.

So after the case was over and Miguel had been returned to his apathetic foster workers, Perdido showed up at the group home with some stock-car-racing tickets. The other kids were green with envy. Then came Saturday boxing and the roller derby and a wilderness-survival weekend and Sundays at the pistol-practice range. Perdido, whose career had never allowed him to marry, became a regular. Over ice cream he'd relive some of his more intrepid exploits for his "godson." Finally the detective began to ask him if he wanted to trade these vicarious kicks for some real action. Miguel decided to join the force.

Miguel slipped back into his briefs, chinos, and short-sleeved white shirt, then began the complicated process of styling his hair. Meanwhile his mentor was still at the desk, resolutely shuffling through photos of victims, looking for features that might match the thing at the pool. A half smile crossed the detective's lips as he thought of his rookie's childish reaction to the stiff. But the boy was climbing back into the saddle. He could hear him sprucing up in the bathroom. The public guardian had to admit that he was more than a little proud of his own talents as a mentor. Miguel was a throwaway kid from a group home. He would have had the dimmest prospects for making it on the force.

Perdido looked down at the photo in his hand of the recently deceased William George Champion. Now here, on the other hand, was a boy who, to all appearances, should have had the brightest future of all.

Who was William George Champion, and how exactly did he fall into the clutches of the maker of the collage monster? The answer to that question lies buried in the distant past.

Champion was Pasadena's most prized junior athlete, the son of a respected businessman known as King Champion. His mother, Beatrice Champion, was a well-liked local TV talk-show hostess in the city of Pasadena.

Trim and golden as an ear of new corn, Champion Junior had known only triumph as a teenager. He was the kind of letter man that parents held up as an example to wayward children. "Why can't you be more like William George Champion?" was a question heard repeatedly in the game rooms of many homes in Pasadena.

Unknown even to Champion himself was a psychic flaw that would later seal his fate. It had been inculcated some fifteen and a half years ago, when Champion's mother, Beatrice, returned from the hospital after rhinoplasty. Only a drop of her own vanity had led to the decision to remake her nose. The decision had been influenced by the growing demand for her popular afternoon talk show.

As she stared into the mirror at her bandaged nose and swollen, blackened eyes, Beatrice's heart began to beat anxiously. It had never occurred to her that she would have to go through this interim period of disfigurement while the surgery healed and set. What bothered her most of all was the idea of her three-month-old infant, William George, being subjected to the monstrous sight. Having had a talk-show guest who explained that bonds between parent and early infant are first established by the "reassuring and tender expression on the face of the mother," Beatrice was deeply worried about her son's conceptualization of her face. Her fears about traumatizing him led her to the memory of a cotton sock.[1]

---

[1]Unorthodox conjugal practices are sometimes at the basis of the most successful marriages. In the early years of their marriage, Beatrice Champion and her husband, King, peppered their intimacies with mari-

To Beatrice, it seemed in the best interests of healthy child rearing to temporarily create a substitute face for the tender infant until the swelling had deflated and the nose had healed. It was an image that she then spent hours forging, basing it upon the advice of the best books on child rearing she could find in the library, and using paint, inks, cosmetics, and color photographs of herself. For approximately two weeks little Champion was treated to a facsimile of his mother's features, frozen in an expression that she considered to be the most receptive and nurturing for a young infant. In short, the development of Champion Junior's self was indelibly marked by this "static" episode in which there were no mobile clues to distinguish among the times when Mommy was pleased or not pleased, ready to come forth with the food, or to abandon, etc.[2]

We come now to Champion's golden-haired teenagehood, the talk of Pasadena, but in some ways merely a graven image, a kind of mirroring of Mommy's synthetic expression, forever fixed in the same monotonous, nurturing mode. Such a history of stunted ego formation makes it no surprise, then, that the lithe-limbed youngster was easy prey for the dissector of Pasadena.

We can imagine him after school on the day it happened, soaring through the air at the track field as was his wont, each tapered, bronzed leg flung rhythmically in front of the

---

tal aids they'd read about in obscure magazines. As an example, they played a "seeing-eye" game in which Beatrice sometimes spent an entire weekend deprived of her sight with the use of various decorative blindfolds and led from couch to table by her husband, whose caresses came at unpredictable moments. This soon developed into a kind of fond foreplay in which King covered her entire face with a cotton stocking fastened at the neck, upon which he drew or pasted new features, referring to her in childish tones as his "Kewpie doll."

[2]The well-meaning Beatrice unfortunately had little familiarity with object-relations theory, which demonstrates how dependent the preverbal child is upon its mother's changing expressions. Even the tiniest infant intently studies a mother's facial gestures in an attempt to build a composite personality from their transformations.

other. Then later, in the locker room, his slender waist creased by a spankingly white towel, William George is gazing intently into the mirror, but perhaps a bit too blankly, wondering who he could be, arranging his still damp locks into a study of insouciance and wishing something magical would happen to him. Meanwhile a car is creeping up to the gymnasium. With book bag slung over one shoulder, Champion leaves the gymnasium and sprints toward home, raising clouds of dust around his coltish ankles. His mind is empty and unformed, like a still pool waiting for the concentric rings of a dropped pebble. The car approaches like a dark phantom, slows down . . . Whether a hypodermic syringe darts suddenly from a sleeve after the boy is drawn into the car by an appeal through a tinted windshield to his yearning for self-discovery, or whether he is later proffered a sugared drink laced with a deranging chemical, no one knows, but something has been loosed behind the mask, something darker and more uncontrollable. Something like an animal.

PSYCHIATRIC EVALUATION

Patient: Wm. G. Champion
Date: November 5, 19--
Source of Referral: Patient was referred by ER, where he was examined yesterday evening.
Presenting Problem: Family complained of extreme irritability, aggression, irrational behavior, etc.

Patient is a healthy-looking teenager of sixteen, Caucasian, dressed in an immaculate, tapered T-shirt and tight blue jeans, brought to me by his terrified and exhausted parents, who had first noticed a mood swing on Sunday evening, November 4, at about six P.M. Later that evening his mother and sister had brought him to the emergency room, where he was denied admission to hospital by examiner who found no PCP or other known hallucinogens in his urine and who referred him to me for the following morning.

On first entering my office, body language indicated a highly disturbed state. I mean to say that movement through space was little more than a series of writhings, fist clenchings, and shoulder hunchings in the manner of the late actor James Dean—a near convulsive expression of defiance, fear, and rage.

Uncertain of how to approach an adolescent in such an exaggerated emotional state, and fearing for my safety, I thought it best to remain as silent as possible during the initial part of the interview. I shrugged off all accusations of a delusional nature and all of his explosions of temper with mute empathy. Finally, toward the end of the first half hour, I managed to extricate a story whose climax would have made a less seasoned professional withdraw in shudders.

It happened yesterday evening when the boy was sent

home from the hospital and presented to his father, who was unaware of the mood change, having returned home late from a ribbon-cutting ceremony for a new branch of his chain of stores, Golden Champion Gear. Once apprised of the situation by mother and daughter, the father expressed categorical disbelief and accused the mother of being overprotective, demanding that the boy be brought before him that instant. Upon seeing the boy in his obviously agitated state, the father suddenly became outraged and categorically refused to hug him after this was suggested, and then repeatedly and tearfully requested, by the mother.

The boy admits then feeling an irresistible urge to show his invulnerability to any intervention—well meaning or not—on the part of his father. He savagely challenged his father to hit him, which was forthcoming in the area of the face. He prodded him to repeat the cuffs on the face, which grew in intensity until the boy's mouth and nose were streaming blood.

Surfacing as if from a trance, the father was filled with horror at the sight of his own handiwork. He fled to the bathroom with the son at his heels, who in smug, dry-eyed silence, watched his father leaning against the sink and weeping.

The father then went to bed without further discussion, sometime after which the boy rose from his own bed, took his father's hunting rifle, cocked it, and went into his parents' bedroom. How much time had elapsed between the beating and this action is unclear. But at present the boy seems to have no sense of any connection between the two incidents. Apparently he held the barrel of the gun for what he suspects was over an hour against his father's sleeping head, until his mother awoke to the scene and begged him in a whisper to hand her the gun. According to the mother (whom I interviewed afterward), the boy then folded up like a released spring and seemed to lapse into a kind of trancelike state. He was taken back to his bed.

Little more was noted during this first interview, aside from certain physical symptoms that undoubtedly have psychosomatic parameters. For example, the boy complained repeatedly of foot cramps, claiming that these were so severe and prolonged and caused such a pronounced downward curvature of the foot that he sometimes had to walk on the tips of his toes, toe walking being an experience he then claimed, paradoxically, to enjoy.

*Hey I can't walk on the soles of my feet anymore, I
can only walk on my toes,[3] they feel springy and heavy
at the same time. Hey my toes are stepping out of the
house all by themselves and into the backyard. Help,
that barking and growling, all of them whirling around
me, making me deaf. Look at the teeth on that one!*

*Wow there are points of teeth at my crotch and hot
breath on my belly. GO AHEAD, EAT ME. I want
you to. That Big One standing at the edge of trees,
pretending not to look at me, must be the leader. What
a snout, it looks enormous and that bloody smell coming from it. It kills me the way that little one leaps up
and begins nipping at the edge of Big One's lips, prying
his jaws apart with her nose, and now she has her
whole head in his mouth. She's gurgling down something coming up from Big One's throat. All the little
ones, too, they're crowded around Big One, except
nobody seems to care about this old hunter, standing
over me with his teeth clamped in my ear. AM I YOUR
SWEETIE, OLD MAN? That smell sliding out of your
mouth, old guy, it smells so yummy that I want to lick
some of it. Those others yelping around us, they won't
hurt me, will they? You want me with you, seems to me.*

*We're running wild, from smell to smell. I love it, I
can learn to know the smells that we want right away.
But now it's getting more mixed, there're all kinds of
other yukky smells that are not so good. Something
twisted keeps us going, though, you just have to! Those
guards that stay at the flanks keep ripping at you! Big
One up there in front with Her isn't even paying a
damn bit of attention to where we're going, he's too*

---

[3]Unlike humans and bears, who walk on their soles, canines can
only walk on their toes.

*into Her and keeps up that zigzagging around Her. I
wish he'd let go of her smell. It isn't right where he's
taking us, these smells getting more and more mixed
up, but I can't stop, I'm just too excited. Big One's
chest's so pumped up, maybe he's mad and wants to eat
us. He keeps whirling around and lunging at the one
behind him and suddenly the whole line has to pull
back squealing surprised.*

*That mind-blowing smell emerging from all the rest!
It's so sweet, it's almost unbearable and now it's turning
into a sound that's earsplitting, as if Big One is laughing at us, making fun of us so we'll throw ourselves
against the boards, rip 'em away. Who cares if the wire
cuts right through our gums. Our mouths are being
bandaged by feathers, the kind that feel good tickling
the back of your throat, making you want to throw up,
feed the young ones—soft, exploding skin and crackling bones, blood spurting out everywhere. I never
thought it would keep going like this. Now I can feel it
wanting to rise back up out of my throat. But I want to
keep it down, I don't want to give any away to the little
ones, it feels so randy—GOD! WHAT WAS THAT?
Something yanking me back, an invisible sharp pull
and then that horrible searing stinging and then blackness.*

FERAL DOGS TIED
TO COOP SLAYINGS

South Pasadena—Last night the third of incidents involving the slaying of farm animals occurred in the Pasadena area between midnight and one A.M., off Sawyer Road at a small chicken coop kept by residents of the Twain Trailer Park. A resident, who identified himself as Phil Android, a breeder, said that he became suspicious when he heard high-pitched wails, screeches, and snarls coming from the area where the coop is. The next morning, it appeared that the coop had been forcibly entered. Some of the sixteen hens had been removed or had escaped into the nearby woods while others lay slain not far from the coop.

What is important about this particular incident is that it provides contradictory evidence to previous theories about the animal killings that have occurred these past three months in the Pasadena area. In all of these cases, human involvement had been assumed. The county examiner's office has suggested that anxiety over the serial disappearance of teenagers in the area may have fueled suspicions that the animal murders were the work of a deranged individual. But on close inspection of the coop, an ASPCA investigator discovered teeth marks on many of the boards. It seems that the boards were ripped off their frames by animals of the canine family. Despite the fact that a canine capable of wrenching the boards out of their frames would have had to have had a jawbone and dentition of superior strength, like a wolf's, wolves and coyotes have been extinct in the Pasadena area, as in most of the West, for over sixty years. Nevertheless, it is now assumed by the ASPCA and the county examiner that some type of canines, probably feral dogs, are responsible for the recent chain of farm-animal killings.

"Think about it," said the detective. "How many of the thoughts that you had at four do you remember? And if you did, would they mean two cents to you? It seems to me that the twist to this particular case lies somewhere in that gray area."

It is nearing midnight in Pasadena, but the sleuths' day is far from over. They're still sitting in the motel room where the body was found, going over and over fragments, trying to piece them together.

"But didn't you tell me," said Miguel, "if I got your earlier explanation of Statute 444 right, that minors got no real thoughts?"

"Oh, they've got 'em, Miguel. They get 'em from their parent or guardian."[4]

"Jeez." The rookie nods dimly.

"I'm convinced," the detective goes on, "that whoever is doing this is specifically interested in the big crossover, when thoughts are passed to you without your knowing it.

"But let's get back to the evidence. We got a lead here, come in this morning, but it could be a dead end. A kid who

---

[4]The voiding of conflictual strain and other troubling psychic material by transference across generations is a social projection of our instinct for species preservation. For those who find themselves entering adulthood with uncharted anxieties or a lack of original purpose, a repository for this debilitating existential burden must be created. Thus, individuals who could drift aimlessly into vagrancy or violence are furnished with an agenda that will carry them through their most potentially dangerous years: it is the production of inheritors.

Inheritors themselves are generally unconscious of their roles as objects of transference during the time that they serve as implantation units for the defense mechanisms of the previous generation. And by the time they discover their legacy, there is little alternative but to pass it down the line. Grandparenthood accordingly represents the most blissful of conditions for any individual anxious to reconstitute repressed conflicts and anxieties in a relocated space, assembly-line-style. In this case the burden has been shunted so far ahead into time and space that only an unfettered and miraculous gratefulness is felt toward the new, largely unknown bearer, finding expression in the phenomenon of "spoiling."

allegedly was abducted and given the drug and then escaped. We got the guy he was accusing, who is some kind of ghetto priest, but we'll probably have to let him go on his own recog while the case is pending. And the kid has gone loony. He's under observation."

Perdido reached into his briefcase to take out the file, which had just been sent over from headquarters.

In the victim's own words:

I was minding my business trotting along Old Mill Pond Road, just watching my shoes raise clouds of dust in front of me. Or maybe I was listening to the cuffs of my corduroys whoosh against each other.[a] Or was I noticing the smell of the new vinyl book bag my mom had given me? School and practice were over, and anticipating what might lie ahead for the evening filled me with excitement. I began to skip. Suddenly a car horn blared, there was the screech of brakes, and I narrowly missed getting my toes squashed by the big black treads of a car tire. When I looked up, I saw the red, angry face of a man[b] cut in two by sunlight hitting his tinted windshield. Since the man I am referring to looked very angry, I hurried to do what I felt was expected of me. I darted around the front of the car to the open window of the driver's seat.[c] My lowered eyes rested on his forearm, which lay on the edge of the

---

[a]Complainant's long trim legs and baggy pants did indeed produce a very noticeable "whooshing" sound.

[b]"My definition of a man is somebody who doesn't look like me, a boy," the complainant would later explain. "For instance, men often have extra skin on their face that tends to hang down from their jaw. Also, a man is not tougher than somebody like me, as is generally claimed, but softer, or flabbier, with his drooping, wrinkled eyes, thick hands (maybe there is a stale smell thinly disguised by mouthwash and shaving lotion coming from somewhere). Everything to do

car door. This part of a man's body, with its sparse hair, is only less disgusting to me than sprouts of hair in the ears and nostrils. I wanted to avoid this sight and immediately looked up, but only to be startled by something in the eyes. Although they were the overexerted yet determined eyes of their kind—riddled by the desire for achievement—there was something jewellike, or unmanlike, about them. Something very much like my own. [d]

I don't remember his exact words. [e] *I only know that somehow I wanted to make up for my foolishness; so when he asked me how to get into town, which was still eight miles away and involved a series of detours around Old Mill Pond because the bridge had collapsed, I eagerly began to supply him with the information (I've always been super at giving directions). But he impatiently waved me still, announcing that there was no way he could keep such a mishmash straight and that I should show him on the map. He told me to climb into the front seat. After he had spread out a large map that covered both our laps, his blunt, hair-sprouting finger began to trace a meandering path*

---

with me is skin stretched tightly over bones. I never huff and puff, it never seems I'm hurrying, no, there is very little about me that resembles a man."

[c]Apparently to apologize to the driver without having to squint into the sun.

[d]Complainant later clarified this remark by explaining: "For some would say that I am a puppet with hard, unchanging eyes made of glass and a face made of the smoothest wood, whereas others call me a boy."

[e]"Why don't you watch where you're going" or "You'll kill yourself if you're not careful," in all likelihood.

through an area I could not place. He began speaking in a singsong voice; I only realized later that he was pronouncing a series of non sequiturs, phrases used to ask and give directions, to orient oneself on a map and discuss it with others.ᶠ Under the map he let the back of his hand, which was bent so that the knuckles protruded, sink more and more emphatically against my thigh, until he slid the hand along the corduroy, then turned it over and clasped my thing through the material.ᵍ Although the car had seemed of average size stopped on the road, the interior now looked enormous, amazingly spacious; the windshield was a blinding pool of light, and the thick, mahogany-rimmed dials of the radio gleamed like the finest silver. When he had unzipped my fly and slipped his fingers under my underwear to take hold of my thing, he placed his other hand under my chin and inserted the tip of his thumb between my lips. And then, without a word, he turned away and began driving.

We seemed to drive for hours, and as we did, the sun gradually sank until there was darkness. I had no idea where we were going, and the landscape seemed more and more unfamiliar. It was as if we had left my neighborhood, the town, the country—I won't say "the world"; soon the roadside was filled with the shadows of foliage I had never seen before: tall, thick, gnarled trees with stubbed, wisp-covered branches, all pointing upward. And then I think there were strange square cactuses

---

ᶠThe exact nature of these utterances can only be imagined.

ᵍComplainant later remembered that this action caused him to glance around the car and notice that the upholstery was especially luxurious; it was made of the richest leather and the carpets were of the thickest pile.

with enormous bulbous leaves. Finally he pulled into a long graveled driveway that he said led to his home, and in the darkness I saw many gables. Two enormous Dobermans came bounding toward the car barking. He opened the door and they leapt in and began to lick his face. They ignored me.

The man's house was all glass, silver, and Lucite. There was very little fabric, and when there was a need for it—for instance, the couches, bed sheets, or towels—it was always a spotless white. This is your new home, he said. It would be impossible for you to leave this place, because if you try, you will only walk into mirrors or bang your head against panes of glass. You will remain naked because you have no need for clothes. When you clean yourself, you will imagine that your body is made of an almost grainless wood, as white as birchwood. Now you exist only to experience pleasure, and any thoughts you have will be as transparent as the prisms in this chandelier above your head. The idea of being a prisoner here left me no regret for my parents, but I did think I might miss my grandparents.

After I had undressed and he had touched my body everywhere, he led me to an enormous white marble table that seemed balanced on a pedestal of glass. And I saw his hands move through the rainbow-studded air to pour a few drops of crystal liquid onto a plate that seemed to be made of silver; then the glistening drops flowed together into a gleaming, pearlescent shape into which he slid the edge of a shiny knife, which sent flashes through the air that lit up parts of his face and his cold, steellike blue eyes. Suddenly the knife soared through the air and his head tilted back. I could see his large, dark, moist nostrils, and the thudding of blood through a cord in his neck, which suddenly looked very powerful as the liquid slipped into his nose and disap-

peared. Now you take some, he said; and as the drops rolled along the cutting edge of the knife toward its tip and the knife flashed toward me, I was afraid it was going to slice my eyes, but the blade slid flat against my nose and the cold liquid was sucked into my nostril as I inhaled, making the whitest light in the world burst through me until I exploded into a million tiny pieces that . . .

Inspector Perdido threw down the report in disgust. "I think we've heard enough of this tripe."

"Jesus," said his rookie assistant, "that kid really knows how to tell a story. My knees got wobbly."

"Even a rookie cop should be able to tell that kid's lying," snapped Perdido drill-sergeant-style. "This reads like it came straight outa Sing Sing—the writing program! The whole thing's like a molester's fantasy, the kind of people this kid is used to pleasing!"

"You mean that isn't what happened?" blurted out the rookie incredulously.

"I would doubt it," said the detective in a sinister voice. "Here's my version. This sounds more like it to me."

I ran away from my fucking asshole of a father because he was always getting drunk and beating up on the old lady. I thought I'd have to walk to town, and then be able to hitchhike to the city by morning, when along comes this fruit in a fancy car, making eyes at me through the open window. "Hello, young man," he lisps, "Do you need a ride?" I get in and right away he's got his hands all over me. Normally I would have smashed his face and taken whatever is in his wallet for doing that, but I really wanted to get out of town before my old man sobered up enough to call the cops on me; so I tell this faggot, listen, not now, I mean, why don't we go to the city and get a room there or something and really have a good time, but we better not try anything here because I'm underage and the people in this town know me. Well, it was the wrong thing to say because immediately this guy starts worrying about the law, wants me to get out of the car, so I put his hand over my dick, and when he feels how big it is, he says okay, okay, then let's go to the city. So in the city he stops at a grocery store and buys two six-packs and we pop 'em open and start drinking. I'm kind of high and the fruit is getting sauced and then he gets his bright idea: hey, we don't have to waste money on a room, I know a place we can drive where there is nobody around, and I think, shit, where the fuck am I going to sleep if he takes off? So I say okay but then you got to pay me, and the faggot says you never said anything about money before. Both of us are making such a hell of a lot of noise that a cop comes up to the car and sticks his flashlight in. And I figure, if they're gonna send me back to that asshole father of mine for a beating because this faggot was too cheap to pay for a room, then let him take some of the consequences . . .

What I remember is that I was all filled up with feathers and blood gurgling in my belly, my nose full of that wild singing smell and sharp yelping in my ears, when something pulls me backward into pain and blackness. And when I wake up, the pain thing is still waiting there for me! I had to do everything it said. Like I would be leaping forward into the bright air, thinking that it's gone, when suddenly the hot pain would rip through me. It began at my neck, then made my legs go stiff.

Or I'd be lying in the sun minding my own business, letting it bake me so that I felt like part of the ground, and suddenly something yanks me up to a standing position, it drags me across the grass to another place, maybe to some hay that smells like urine. The creaking of metal, I had to stay there until I felt the yank again. The worse part was when there was a smell that I got into, it went inside me so that it seemed like a sound and told me what to do. I'd let it run me forward toward the next smell, and then suddenly: the horrible pain again, ripping me away from it, fighting to be stronger than the smell and winning.

By the time this clenched fist was held out for me to

lick, I was trained and ready to do anything, bowing down to the salty taste of the hairless skin and licking it to show that I would follow it and live under it, rubbing against the thigh because I'd begun to realize who was the master of my pain. And then just one time, right before the pain came, I happened to turn around to try to see who—or what—did it. I saw a man in a black raincoat holding out a steel rod attached to a wire, moving it toward my neck. He was wearing a collar too. No, not that kind. I think it was a clerical collar.

PART
II

The ghost-plagued television crackled with static, making the commentator's voice seem two-dimensional.

"The story you are about to see may not be a reality in your city. But thousands of miles away, it is daily fare for the many children who must live it . . ."

The scene dissolved to a tropical setting, palm trees in still air over a litter-strewn street. Beneath one of the trees, a heap of dirty cardboard began to stir.

"Here is Pepe, age twelve, waking up under his piece of cardboard. He's had to fight off the other boys huddled against him for warmth all night to keep them from stealing it. He's searching his pocket for his tiny pebble of crack, or freebase, and his tinfoil pipe. It will help to wake him up and stave off the usual morning hunger. He'll be stashing it away quickly before the police come by for the daily sweep . . .

"Pepe and his friends are on their way to a garbage dump near the city limits, where nonbiodegradable fragments—bottle caps, razor blades, and plastic bags—can be salvaged from the decomposing organic garbage. If enough of these scraps can be found, he might be able to trade them for a few pennies worth of food at the market . . .

"It has not been a very profitable day at the dump. And, unfortunately, weeks of wading in the compost heap have infected Pepe's legs. Further contact with the enzymes is painful, obviously, and tends to inflame the sores . . .

"This is Pepe's friend, eleven-year-old Tito. He is showing Pepe his new clothes and the silver lighter they will use to smoke the crack they will share. Tito is explaining that he has met a rich Belgian tourist who likes to buy him presents. Maybe Pepe would like to meet him too . . ."

Insomniacs who watched these events dramatized on a late-night television show rushed to their checkbooks with sighs of relief when the appeal to support the faraway mission came on. The program had been especially rending, since it purported to use as actors the actual children to whom these events had occurred.

Checks written out, lights were turned off with the reassuring feeling that one's own children would never be subjected to a similar horror. God willing, they would always
be protected by loving parents and grandparents, right-
minded teachers, or charismatic law enforcers. In this
city, children were neither a useful product for the work
force, nor a drain on the economy, but a luxury, something
to be cultivated into masterpieces of which the creator
could be proud.

Things looked different in a seedier part of town, where a
balding, disheveled priest watched the broadcast on a flop-
house TV. He was a man who knew this tale well, a man
who had spent the greater part of his life in the thick of
it.

Father Bob wasn't a bad man, but perhaps one who
expected too much from this world below. He was a man
who equated the act of putting innocent flesh to its ordinary
trials and tribulations with subjecting it directly to the gap-
ing jaws of evil. And try as he might to resist, he always
found himself succumbing to the temptation of face-to-face
confrontations with the process.

His eyes left the television to rest on the bony figure
passed out on the bed. Through the window curtains lying
dead in the stale air, blue neon from the sign outside the
window illuminated the blunt young face. Father Bob had a
vision of snowy wings framing the surly mouth and dark-
circled eyes. Then he remembered that the boy's name was,
ironically, Angel.

In boys like Angel the priest took the opportunity to
uncover many layers of his own psyche. He realized that he
had always wondered, for example, why those with the least
interest in the future—teenagers—were assigned to be its
harbingers—a fate they claimed to revile but later embraced.
Father Bob also wondered why full consciousness of their
own secret longings and elastic physicalities was denied certain individuals by terrified others who insisted they serve as

epitomes of purity and ineffectuality. In short, Father Bob was an idealist who yearned to free teenagehood from its enslavement; rescue it from its prefabricated, labeled state; return to it its Edenic vitality. But all his efforts had only succeeded in drawing out animality and violence.

The priest woke Angel up.

He stretched. As a street person he knew how to enjoy the luxury of a real mattress, but ingrained caution made him stop in the middle of his relaxed movement when he felt Father Bob's eyes resting on him. Jerking to a sitting position, Angel lit a cigarette and began watching the story of the abandoned children on the snowy television screen.

"I gotta go," he mumbled.

"But you've hardly rested," said Father Bob. "And I haven't even told you about the club."

"What club?" said the boy.

Father Bob averted his eyes and did not answer. He had spent years studying the insecurities of people like his listener and knew all about their need to belong. Their fear of being ostracized could lead them into hierarchies that they would not question. What is more, their yearning for an identity gave them a special attraction to the aura of the secret society, especially if it involved handshakes, passwords, ceremonies, and the like.

"First I have to know I can trust you," said Father Bob. "The club's a secret."

The boy nonchalantly took a puff on the cigarette and blew smoke rings into the air. His face lapsed into an affectation of apathy, but Father Bob thought he saw a spark of interest beneath the wolfish street cynicism. "I won't tell nobody," the boy said. "Has it got something to do with boosting—electronic equipment or something?"

"Much more exciting," said Father Bob, trailing one finger through the dust on the night table.

The boy's eyes grew wider. "You mean pushing?"

"No," said the priest. "More powerful."

"Pimping?"

"No. Mind control."

"What is that supposed to be?" The boy started to get up.

"It takes awhile to understand," said Father Bob, gently forcing him back down, and from his pocket he produced a ring. He held it up into the flashing blue neon. "Do you like this?"

"Yeah, it's really fresh," said Angel, reaching to touch the silver-wolf carving on it. "Can I have it?"

"It's part of the initiation ceremony," said the priest, "for the club. We all have rings like this." Raising his other hand into the neon light, he showed the boy the ring on his finger, identical to the first.

Angel took the first ring and began turning it over in his fingers. "What's this club about?"

"Tell me about your parents," countered Father Bob in a casual tone.

Angel looked away, stared at the fuzz on the television screen now that the station had gone off the air. "Lasts I heard about her, she was with her sister in South Pasadena. Him, I don't know where he is. I hope I never run into him 'cause I'll kick ass if I do."

"What does any parent really know about his children," said Father Bob with a sigh.

The boy's ears pricked up.

"Parents are the last people to know what's best for you," the priest went on.

"You're telling me?" said Angel with a glint of appreciation in his eyes.

"Teachers too," said the priest. "Don't listen to them."

"Hey," said Angel enthusiastically, "what is this club, anyway? You haven't told me yet. Are you the leader, kind of like the don? What do you deal in?"

"Souls," said the priest.

"*Souls?*" Since Father Bob was not wearing his clerical collar, the boy burst out laughing. He slapped one thigh, and the mattress made a creaking sound. "Souls! Are you some kind of religious nut?" He tried to stand up.

"Wait!" Father Bob's voice was stern now. "By souls I mean an entire mentality, not some outdated hocus-pocus. I'm talking about consciousness here, everything that's been stuffed into your head since you were old enough to see and hear." He leapt up, shut the window, turned off the television. "I want to show you something. See that ring you're still holding? Open it up. The top part opens."

Angel bent over the ring and tugged on the silver wolf. It fell open with a tiny ping, and immediately Father Bob held a saucer under it. Drops of a crystalline liquid fell onto the saucer.

Father Bob scooped the drops onto the edge of a knife, then quickly held the knife close to the boy's nose. "Smell," he said. Immediately the boy's eyelids closed. His head lolled sideways.

Grim anticipation coiled in Father Bob's belly. What better frame of mind for the preparation of instruction was there than one in which the subject was hypnotically open to influence? For influence can only enter the mind as a drop of water will enter a moist sponge.[5]

As the boy's head dipped backward one more time, Father Bob gently pulled him to a standing position. He began to drag the limp body, which slumped against him, through a kind of fox-trot, humming "Fascination." Then suddenly the boy straightened and began leading, jerkily, on the tips of his toes. Movement through space became more stylized, extended into writhings. Now he hunched his shoulders and pulled back his loins in spasm; his arms were flung up and back as if nailed there. A stony look transfixed the eyes.

An intensely pure tenderness welled up inside Father Bob as he swept the boy to the bed. The youngster lay stiff and arched on it, without moving. Perhaps, hoped the priest, he had him in a pure state now, and this time the subject would not lapse into animality.

Slowly and methodically he began his implantation.

---

[5]Ignatius Loyola, *Spiritual Exercises*

A hope for saving other runaways from a similar fate rested on a new technology just purchased by the Pasadena Police Department. It is called "computer aging." Designed according to the latest research in aging factors, it involves feeding an image of the lost child from a photograph into a computer with graphic capabilities. The image can then be systematically "aged," with input from environmental factors, to produce a picture of the child as he or she might look at the current time.

When the Bureau of Missing Persons in Pasadena acquired the device, it already had been tested extensively by the Atlanta Police Department. What is more, a less complex model was being employed by psychotherapists who worked with the bereft parents of long-term runaways. Many of these people were still plagued by the image of a beloved face frozen in time, even though the face may have long ago evolved into that of an unimaginable individual. Now, before them on a color CRT, a gracefully matured image of their little boy or girl materialized—sturdier chinned and longer nosed but perhaps with the same vulnerable expression in the eyes and the same unconscious expression in the parted lips. The patient then engaged in imaginary dialogue with the screen as one step in the wrenching process of disinvolvement.

Most recently, computer aging is being put to wider applications. It was mass-marketed as a program for home computers, and those fearful of the ravages of time upon their looks hoped to use the program to second-guess the aging process. But for this it proved unnecessarily demoralizing.

Now it is rapidly taking hold as an educational tool. In some of our nation's more prestigious academic institutions, a child entering school for the first time receives an image of himself upon successful graduation, with proper weight and height gains, intellectual achievement, and character maturations printed out below. A duplicate is sent home to parents, and the image is used by teachers for instructional modeling of the development of the child.

Nine P.M. In their bungalow in the Pasadena hills, Perdido and his rookie were getting ready to climb into their twin beds. For the past few moments the detective had been congratulating himself for his perseverance, which led to his matchup of six photos of teenage corpses with the face of the corpse at the pool. Only the chin of the body at the pool, which seemed to belong to a Caucasian, did not match the Negroid skin tones of the corpse on which that particular feature was missing.

Miguel was pulling on shorty pajamas. He turned down the covers and hopped into bed. Tonight he was filled with silent admiration for the patient sleuthing talents of his mentor; maybe being a rookie was not half that bad after all. He settled into his pillow and was overtaken suddenly by a sense of having a personal stake in this case. He could almost feel it pressing in around him with an enchanting yet dangerous intimacy. He gazed at his mentor for reassurance, but the sight of Detective Perdido in yellow pajamas turning down his covers mysteriously accelerated the nervous, intimate feeling. Pushing against the sheets with his toes, he realized that they had been pulled in too tightly. He suppressed an impulse to ask Mr. Perdido to get up and loosen them, even though memories of being "tucked in" by the detective did not reach far into the past. He hopped out of bed and loosened the hospital corners himself.

"Got ants in your pants?"

"I hate to be constrained, Mr. Perdido, maybe 'cause when's I was little, this foster mom I had for a while was always putting me in one of those harnesses—you know, the kind with a strap attached so you can't run too far."

"A mom's got a lot invested in a kid," mused Perdido.

Because tomorrow would probably prove as grueling as today had been, neither detective nor rookie were anxious for their usual ritual of lights-out immediately, barracks style. Instead Perdido opened a copy of a favorite book,

Adventures of Huckleberry Finn. He began to read it aloud, after reminding Miguel that this was the story of the very first American runaway. But after a while it was obvious to each that the thoughts of the other kept returning to the case.

"Are nigger chins less dark than the rest of their faces?" Perdido asked.

"How should I know?"

"I thought all Colombians were supposed to be part Negro."

Miguel considered the truth of the supposition in light of his alien appendage, but sleep mercifully took hold of him. He drifted into a dream about his onetime foster mother, Georgia, a model, and her sister, Betty, a photographer.

"You lift his legs over his head while I wipe. Yuk! I should have done this an hour ago."

(All flipping upside down. Leg things flying away from me.)

"Now help me turn him, will you, Betty? Fiddlesticks, he's going to need a bath after all. Will you get that tub again? And fill it up halfway. Stick your elbow in."

(Jiggles.) The pink tube growing.

"Ain't we cute. Stop touching that nasty thing. C'mon, let's see a smile now. Let Aunt Betty give you a kiss."[6]

---

[6]The curious phenomenon of slobber kissing (coinage: U. Molinaro) has served as a point of juncture whereby procreatively inactive members of the extended family become tangentially engaged in the libidinal thrust of generation. Certain zones of a minor's body are designated as the legitimate field for slobber kissing. In most contexts these include the cheeks, neck, and top of the head, but rarely the lips; whereas in settings where partial undress is considered normal—such as the beach—the arms, chest, abdomen, and, in the case of very young children, even the bottom are included. Although the sudden and sometimes unexpected assault of wet lips on most of these areas would be considered prosecutable or at least a public embarrassment when the object is an adult; individuals who have not attained majority often have extensive

(Jiggling.)

"Okay. Up we go and in we go."

Help. (Bleeding or melting.)

"C'mon, angel, the water's not going to bite you. Stop whimpering."

Help.

"Betty, hold the edge of this tub."

Draining away.

"There now. Everybody likes a bath."

Push back again. Here we go. (Melting again.)

"Darn. He's peeing. He's too full of liquids. Hand me that Q-tip."

Here it comes, mouth.

"Don't grab at it! Stop biting it! Oh! you're splashing me! Bad, bad, li'l boy."

That stick so loud? Should swallow it.

"Stop it! Do you hear me! That's a good fella. Now just a little shampoo. Look, isn't he adorable, Betty! Get the camera. This one's not to be missed. Let's give him the duck. Hurry, before he starts splashing again."

(Stabbed.)

"Okay, only one more shot, I think the flash frightened him."

(Stabbed.)

---

experience as the object of slobber kissing, intimate familiarity with the smell of Aunt Heidi's White Shoulders or Uncle Morton's gum disease being the rule rather than the exception. During the period of slobber kissing, the above-named zones become communal property of the extended family, thereby being put at the service of those individuals not fortunate enough to have created their own generational transference units (see footnote 4, page 143), e.g., maiden aunts, bachelor uncles, unmarried sisters, widows and widowers). In rare cases the odors and other sensations experienced by the object during slobber kissing become cathected and take on libidinal associations that influence one's adult search for mates.

"That flash really did frighten him. You're not angry at me, are you, cuddles?"[7]

---

[7]Fully repressed by Miguel was the fact that the sisters sometimes amused each other at home by setting up and shooting novelty poses, which they occasionally offered for sale: When Betty sees the coil of clothesline lying on the table near the tub, she just can't resist. Sneaking up on Georgia from behind, she throws her expertly to the floor. Georgia's legs go kicking into the air, but before she has time to right herself, Betty gets astride her. "Yahoo! Get along, little horsie!" Working expertly against Georgia's kicking, gartered legs, she begins to bind her. Several turns of rope around wrists and waist are enough to lash them tightly together. Her stockinged thighs are bound together by turns of rope just above the knees and just below them, as are her ankles and delicate little feet. Finally Betty takes a smaller length of rope and attempts to tie Georgia's neck to her heels, but Georgia can slip out of it by pressing her feet together. So Betty gets an extension cord to tie the neck and feet. When she has finished, Georgia is ingeniously bound from throat to insteps. Betty delightedly shoots the pose at various interesting angles keeping in mind the enthusiasms of a few faithful customers.

The rookie awoke, blinking perplexedly at the sun stream-ing into the room through the blinds. What was the meaning of his strange dream? Did it hold a clue to the case of the curse on the teenagers of Pasadena?

There wasn't much time to think about that. It had to be after five A.M. already. Miguel could hear the slap of Detec-tive Perdido's razor against the strop and smell his shaving soap. The sensations filled him with a sense of helpless excitement. Once more, for reasons he couldn't express, he felt the case all around him, daring him to reach out to its solution, which Miguel imagined as a kind of soft underbelly that seemed alternately poisonous and yielding.

Heart beating rapidly, he hopped out of the twin bed and glanced around the blue room, letting his eyes rest on Mr. Perdido's gleaming regulations parked heel against heel be-neath the blue-and-yellow curtains with their rodeo motif. The detective's worn badge case lay open on top of the dresser, next to Miguel's new one.

Miguel picked up his badge and walked to the mirror with it. Still in his shorties, he practiced whipping the case out and flipping it open. Then he began his precise routine of dressing, tucking his button-down shirt into his high-pulled Jockey briefs for a smoother fit, and adjusting the waistband of his black chinos so that the crease passed right to the top of his shoes.

Fifteen minutes later and too nervous to eat, he sat inhal-ing the scent of the detective's Old Spice over bacon and eggs in their breakfast nook. Perdido handed him a photo-graph of a twelve-year-old boy.

"Routine work," said the detective through tightened lips, "but important. Hightail it over to Missing Persons and run this through the computer ager. The kid disappeared four years ago, and I want to see if his could have been the chin on that thing we saw yesterday by the pool. Throw a little more down on the cheeks, tighten up the jaw." He tossed Miguel a small key. "This'll get you into the computer room."

Detective Perdido stayed seated in the breakfast nook until he heard Miguel start his car and pull out of the driveway. Then he rose and gently parted the curtains. He watched the car snake down the curving road toward downtown Pasadena.

Sending the boy on assignment always filled him with a tingly feeling. It was like the mixture of pride and trepidation a kid feels when he sets a windup toy on the floor for the first time, points it in the optimum direction, and lets go.

The thought of a windup toy always reminded him of the first one he had as a kid. It was an acrobat in a silver leotard that did somersaults when you wound it up. He could see the toy leaping high above the faded rag rug and all the way up onto the edge of a bed. The woman lying on the bed fumbled to remove her satin sleep mask when she felt the toy land on her, sat up, and squinted into the afternoon light. It illuminated her platinum finger-curls, making them look almost transparent.

As if it were happening again, Perdido felt the surge of joy that came whenever Mom finally woke up. She would always send him to the medicine cabinet over the sink in their trailer for her "medicine," after which he was allowed to play and make noise. Sometimes this didn't happen until the sun was setting, so Perdido spent the day sitting next to the bed and fantasizing that Mom was a sleeping beauty waiting for a prince to revive her.

Then, finally, she'd get out of bed, drink the magic potion he'd brought her, glance at a picture of a man in tights and waxed mustache standing near a trapeze—who was supposed to be Perdido's father—and go behind the screen in their trailer. She'd emerge from it all dressed up in a spangled bathing suit and fishnet stockings, her platinum hair studded with rhinestone pins.

Mom had a dog act, and mother and son followed a traveling carnival in their little trailer. Perdido had loved the mutts; he could almost feel their wet noses nuzzling his ankles.

But he'd had enough of reminiscing. He'd lost an hour already, and he had a case out there to solve. Slipping his badge into his pocket, he walked briskly to his own car and headed for headquarters. He wanted to take another look at the file on that priest.

By the time he got there, the file was gone.

At Missing Persons, Miguel had gingerly made his way down the half-lit hallway, overly conscious of the squeak of his rubber soles on the tiled floor. Missing Persons wouldn't be open for another hour, and he could see through the glass window that the computer room was dark. He tried to create a mental picture of the room, searching his mind for the location of the light switch. Ever since he'd been a little kid, he'd hated stumbling around in the dark, looking for the lights.

He took out the key Detective Perdido had given him and inserted it, but before he could turn it, the door swung open with a creaking sound. Someone had broken the lock.

Miguel stuck a hand into the darkness and began feeling along the wall for the switch. He kept his eyes on an eerie shaft of green light that shot from the shadowy forms of electronic equipment. Finally his fingers felt the switch, and the overhead fluorescent lights fluttered on.

The green glow had been coming from the dials of the computer ager. Whoever had last used it had left it on. Miguel could hear a high-pitched whine coming from the machine. The green light—its diskette light—indicated that whoever had been using it had forgotten to remove their diskette as well.

Miguel pushed the eject button and nothing happened. He tried to turn the machine off, but the on/off button didn't work either.

The rookie felt his palms sweating again, and a cramp retracted his scrotum. Would the detective think he'd botched a routine job? Who had been there before him and broken in? Nervously he opened the shutter door to see if he could spot a jam. Then, using the key to the office, he gently picked at the diskette, which suddenly came popping out.

Looking back on the episode, Miguel wondered why he had decided to put the diskette back into the machine and see what was on it. At the time he thought he was just being thorough, like Detective Perdido would have been. Or maybe he wanted to put the finger on whoever had broken into the place and left the machine in such a state. The diskette made a whirring sound and the rookie pressed "Initial Image."

A balding, middle-aged man's face came on the screen. The dark, watery eyes seemed to belie the vulnerable, pouting expression of the mouth. Miguel pressed the plus button and nothing happened. Sliding his finger to the right, he pressed minus. The machine clicked and moaned. The face disappeared from the screen and returned, looking more youthful. The eyes were brighter, and the jowls hung less loosely at the jawline. Now Miguel understood why the machine had jammed. Somebody had been trying to make the ager go *backward.* He pressed the minus button again. The machine moaned once more, eclipsing the image and replacing it with the same face, even younger. Now more hair sprouted at the crown of the head, and the eyes seemed to challenge. He pressed minus again, and this time the eyes had softened. They were larger looking. Thick, shiny curls framed the face, whose fuller lips rested in a shy, almost guilty pout. Paradoxically, it was not until this teenage image came on the screen that Miguel realized where he had seen the first adult face before. There was something about the teenage image that evoked the man better than his present picture. It was the priest who had been brought in for questioning.

An hour later Miguel sat in the Hyundai, tremblingly holding the photo of the missing boy that Perdido had given him for the computer ager. He'd been so overwhelmed by his identification of the priest that he'd forgotten to put the photo on the machine. Instead he'd dashed over to headquarters and surreptitiously grabbed the file on Father Bob. He was determined to interview Father Bob alone, despite what he knew Perdido would say about sober craft and good sleuthing judgment. If the interview did lead to something, he wouldn't be in for anything but praise.

Miguel looked down at the photo of the twelve-year-old once more and shuddered. The sloe-eyed, rosy-cheeked kid had been missing for four years and was probably dead. It counted as one more child sacrifice. If his disappearance had anything to do with this case, he owed it to this kid and to kids like him to take a few risks. This had become a children's crusade.[8]

Before long, Miguel had left Pasadena and its suburbs. Gradually the roadside was filled with the shadows of foliage he had never seen before, and he felt as if he had left the neighborhood, the town, and even the country.

The strange landscape seemed to take him into another plane. His usually sweaty palms and the butterflies in his stomach were replaced by a floating feeling. It was as if he were traveling vertically, higher or deeper, instead of

---

[8]*Children's crusade*—one manifestation of a popular pietist movement, beginning in the second decade of the thirteenth century. The movement is thought to have been fueled by an impulse of the rural lower echelon to burst the bonds of clerical and noble hegemony. In addition to thirty thousand children, numerous shepherds, tradesmen, and other rural poor took part in the movement, which at times resembled a pillaging rampage. Some of the child participants met an unexpected fate. They were, allegedly, sold into slavery or concubinage upon reaching the coast of North Africa.

driving straight ahead. As he drove, images of his life alternated with details from the case. He saw himself worriedly fingering his member in the shower, then gazing into turquoise water that suddenly became filled with vomit; he was watching with excited envy how the intrepid Detective Perdido bullied a shady motel owner for information, then kicking and screaming as Georgia lowered him into a tub; finally he imagined himself as a newborn infant wailing with hunger in a dark house in a strange country, above which floated the face of the priest as a teenager, an almost sacrificial tenderness in his sad eyes. Somehow this puzzle fit together, but how? It was an insane patchwork, like the Frankenstein-like corpse that had been lying by the pool.

It was getting dark already. The trees had become smudges in the sky. Miguel was turning up a long, graveled driveway. The sight of the black, sharply pointed gables of the house made his head swim pleasurably. His mind almost blank, he left the car, flanked by the two Dobermans that had suddenly appeared at his side. He entered the house without knocking. Light coming from every direction stung his eyes. It was as if the black-and-white tile floor were spinning, carrying him sensually down one Lucite-and-silver corridor and then another. Finally he was standing before the priest, who looked as he had in the first age-reduced image, an attractive man in his early thirties, with clear eyes and a full head of hair. He was wearing a kimono bathrobe, the kind a bachelor would wear.

"It would be impossible for you to leave this place," the priest began to intone in a hypnotic voice like a fortune-teller in a TV movie Miguel had once seen. "You now exist only to experience pleasure, and any thoughts you have will be as transparent as the prisms in this chandelier above your head."

"Cut the crap!" barked the rookie, struggling to regain control of himself and making an effort to reproduce Perido's hard-boiled tone. "Just tell me one thing. What's a priest doing in a groovy bachelor pad like this?"

"Everything exists in conflict with something else. All teenagers know that," answered the priest in a tone of great gravity. " 'Freedom without responsibility'; 'Protect me but keep your distance'; 'Save me but let me struggle!' "

"Why'd you foul up that computer ager?"

"I thought, foolishly," answered the priest with a sentimental sniffle, "about traveling back and starting over again to understand it better. But I got stuck like this."

"Then Detective Perdido was right. It was you who tried to build the perfect teenager."

"When that didn't work, I thought the answer lay in nature," said the priest, gesturing grandly around him.

For the first time Miguel noticed that they weren't alone. A low-pitched growling came from the edges of the room. Draped on the Lucite-and-white furniture and slouched in corners were some of the boys whose pictures he'd seen at Missing Persons. But they looked different now. The hair on their heads and eyebrows had thickened, their jawlines had narrowed into snouts, and they stood balanced on the tips of their toes. Miguel recognized the boy whose picture he had, but now sharp teeth protruded from his mouth, and his eyes were narrowed into suspicious slits. He hissed half consciously at Miguel, then leaned back drowsily against the glass wall.

"They all became animals," the priest went on. "I couldn't implant anything."

Miguel's hands fluttered to his pocket in search of his badge. He flipped it out and displayed it to the priest. "I'm taking you in!"

"Forgive me for disobeying you," said the priest. "Though I have little belief in the authority of your profession, I have

the deepest respect for the prerogatives unjustly denied
your age group."

Suddenly the pack of boys sprang snarlingly into action.
Miguel was surrounded. They began to drive him down a
flight of stairs to the basement.

Could it be that the owner of this Lucite-and-glass house, this jailor of wereboys, was also the possessor of a mysterious laboratory, a place where chemical—and alchemical—miracles were performed? The possibility had never occurred to the rookie. He'd overlooked a crucial clue: the strange crystalline liquid that seemed to alter mind and body.

Surrounded by a kind of vicious, sensual guard made up of the fanged wereboys, Miguel stood gawking at bubbling beakers and alembics in Father Bob's basement laboratory. A viscous, whitish substance dribbled from the spout of one alembic into a graduated cylinder.

Coming out from the tangle of test tubes and piping, the priest held up two gels, quivering in their beakers. "In one beaker are the child's thoughts and in the other is his flesh," he explained.

Apparently the first gel consisted of nervous tissue in which were imprinted adolescent thoughts, longings, and dreams, a task that had taken Father Bob the entire previous week. The other vial, which had a plasmatic, almost iridescent cast, contained the raw material of young flesh, a purified tensor for thoughts and longings.

"This method is far superior to the last two," said the priest. "Piecing together stereotypically wholesome body parts or trying to purify the teenage mind were both grave errors, I now realize. No amount of hacking, sewing, or dosing could ever have brought me the results I'm looking for."

The priest poured the two gels into a crucible. They did not mix, but each time they bumped together, they trembled. He picked up a graduated cylinder full of a white stuff.

"All that remains is the union of the two gels by the addition of a few drops of the binding catalyst—which is a kind of parent in a jar—to create the invincible culture," he explained.

The wide-eyed rookie remained rooted in place.

The priest raised the cylinder and measured two drops into the crucible. The gels became turgid, entwining in a kind of spiral that caused the crucible to rattle. A striated glow pervaded the substance, flickering between gray, rose, and brown, as if in search of the elusive tones of flesh. Miguel wondered what orthopedic object would emerge from the humors, what fragmented body. Would it have the motor skills of a newborn? Or the fully coordinated grace of another Champion?[9]

An intact yet ghostlike image of a teenager streamed from the mouth of the crucible and hovered above it. The priest curiously extended a hand, but to his chagrin, his arm passed right through it. Flickering in and out of vision, the image began to speak.

"O evil, deluded man. Give up your tacky experiments and let me rest for eternity. An unholy pact doomed me to insubstantiality. But your wacky potions and spells called me back into a half existence. Take heed, for you are once again on the brink of a stupid criminal mistake."

Swirling as if made of water, the image continued.

"Poison did this to me. I began my life just like you did. Fragments of a body—arms, hands, eyes—seemed mysteriously to supply my every need. You know the scenario. When I awoke, food was there to satisfy my hunger. When I felt like burping, there was a hand patting my back, etc. I grew accustomed to the service, then terrified of losing it. How could I have guessed that they'd put something in the food?

"So, almost before I knew it, my nights became a purgatory. I was racked by run-of-the-mill, uncontrollable longings. Bitter thoughts of revenge against Mummy and Daddy stung me as well. My deranged mind told me that in the

---

[9]Probably the latter if Father Bob's theoretical basis for his experiment concurred with the ideas of French historian Philippe Aries, who maintained that the children of medieval Europe were indistinguishable from adults in every important way, being regarded merely as adults in miniature. (Philippe Aries, *Centuries of Childhood,* translated from the French by R. Baldick, 1962, Jonathan Cape)

name of protection I was being humored, deceived, intimi-
dated, cajoled, and betrayed. But I kept on swallowing
more because I was polluted. My hunger and the food that
had been forced on me had become identical.

"Above all I somehow knew that I was never to reveal
the cause of my night tortures to those very beings who
might have implanted them. So I kept changing the sheets
and Mummy never knew. The masquerade continued and
my punishment increased. The greatest burden was the feeling that I was now charged with all that was desirable and
that at the same time its fruition was forbidden. To rev
myself up even more, I would fantasize my fragmentation in
the future into the plane of power that had instigated all this
suffering. I dreamed of being just like Dad.

"Finally abuse broke the vicious round. My jailers, who
were seized with longing, committed the ultimate transgres-
sion. At night when my pains were raging, they appeared
before me in unfragmented form. The effect of this was
horrible. As soon as the fragments assumed a definite shape,
I became a cannibal and was simultaneously tormented by
the image of my own body laid out on a table for culinary
purposes. To avoid that fate I attempted suicide. I was
punished for this by being forced to assume the form in
which you now see me."

Miguel, and even the wereboys, listened transfixed, their
mouths hanging open and their eyes wide as saucers. Father
Bob was staring at the image with a tragic, almost exalted
fascination. Then a cleft appeared, a kind of slit that, opening ever wider, threatened to make the image disappear. It
was the only weapon of this passive, powerless entity, a
vortex opening wider and wider. As if in a wind tunnel,
Miguel felt himself being sucked toward it. "Help me!" he
shrieked to Father Bob, his hair blowing about his ears. "I'll
do anything you say!"

But Father Bob had been pulled off his feet and turned
topsy-turvy. First his feet and then the rest of his body were
sucked into the orifice.

The imago loomed like a rubbery doughnut. It slithered out of the crucible and turned into a pool on the floor.

Miguel saw that the wereboys had fallen back into their trance. A shudder passed over him at the sight of their hollow eyes, which stared perplexedly at what had become a pool of plasma on the floor. He drew back with a sigh of relief as he heard Detective Perdido and a squadron of police barreling down the stairs. What had ever made him think he wanted to become a cop?

Evening falls once more in Pasadena, but one unlike any other in the past few months. It is a special night for the city's mothers and fathers, the first in many months when dads can confidently toss car keys to children or send them off in their pajamas into the dark streets to slumber parties. The case of the curse on the teenagers of Pasadena has been solved.

In their quaint home in the hills of Pasadena, Detective Perdido is once more getting ready to turn in for the night. Since today is Wednesday, he does forty brisk sit-ups and push-ups in the living room before changing into his pajamas. Then he sprints breathlessly into the bedroom and finds his rookie, who is to be awarded for his bravery by being raised to the rank of officer tomorrow, standing over a suitcase.

"Goin' somewhere?"

"I didn't have the nerve to tell you, Mr. Perdido. But I figured, well, that maybe it was time I lived on my own, don't you think? I'll be moving into the Mark Twain Trailer Park with a roommate tonight. Name's Android. He's a breeder, and I was wondering if I should look into the field."

Tight-lipped, the detective turns his back on the rookie and marches deliberately into the bathroom. As the boy continues to pack, he can hear him gargling with mouthwash. The detective comes out with a bright smile pasted on his face.

"How's about a kiss?"

"Huh?"

"I said, how about a kiss good-bye . . . Officer."

Miguel hops over his suitcase, plunges into the policeman's arms, and rests there, in safety, just for a moment.

LITERARY ORIGINALS

☐ **THE CARNIVOROUS LAMB by Augustin Gomez-Arcos.** A shocking, irresistably erotic tale filled with black humor. Into a shuttered house, haunted by ghosts of past rebellions and Franco's regime, Ignatio is born. His mother despises him; his failed father ignores him; his older brother becomes his savior, his confidant . . . his lover. Their forbidden relationship becomes the center of this savagely funny, stunningly controversial novel. (258200—$6.95)

☐ **EQUAL DISTANCE by Brad Leithauser.** Danny Ott, a young Harvard law student on leave in paradoxical Japan of Zen masters and McDonalds, plans to "grow up" and "accomplish" things in his year abroad. But when he meets another young American, Greg Blaising, who introduces him to the irresistable neon nightlife of Kyoto, Danny's plans are increasingly upset. Then along comes Carrie. . . . "Constantly surprising, tender and exact." —*Newsweek* (258189—$6.95)

☐ **SELF-HELP: Stories by Lorrie Moore.** In these nine stories Lorrie Moore probes relationships we all recognize, giving poignant, but wickedly funny advice on "How to Be an Other Woman," "How to Talk to Your Mother (Notes)," "How to Become a Writer," and on surviving other modern crises of loss and love by finding the absurd humor at life's core. "Brisk, Ironic . . . Scalpel-sharp."—*New York Times Book Review* (258219—$6.95)

☐ **FARAWAY PLACES by Tom Spanbauer.** Jacob Joseph Weber's childhood days are shattered when a forbidden swim in the river makes him witness a brutal murder. An evocative coming-of-age novel, a brilliantly moving story of hypocrisy, greed and revenge in America's heartland. "Hypnotizing!"—*The New York Times* (262216—$6.95)

☐ **RIVER ROAD by C.F. Borgman.** Eugene Goessler is a man on a journey across the country in search of romantic adventure, both straight and gay, artistic and erotic, psychological and intellectual. "Beautiful writing . . . one of the major gay novels of the year."—*New York Native* (263042—$8.95)

Prices slightly higher in Canada.

Buy them at your local

bookstore or use coupon

on next page for ordering.

Ⓟ   (0452)

Ⓟ **Plume**

COMING OF AGE